Star Crossed

Worlds Apart

STAR CROSSED

Worlds Apart

JOLENE POOLE

TENTH STREET PRESS

THIS EDITION

© Copyright 2013 Jolene Poole

Published by Tenth Street Press   2013

Original cover design by Tenth Street Press

ISBN: 0-9923861-0-1

ISBN13: 978-0-9923861-0-8

This book is a work of fiction. Events and characters mentioned are both of actuality and of the author's invention. Any similarity to persons living or dead is entirely coincidental.

PRINTED IN THE U.S.A.

TENTH STREET PRESS Ltd.
MELBOURNE LONDON
www.tenthstreetpress.com
Email:contact@tenthstreetpress.com

She could hear them creeping down the hall. They were making their way to her room. She would have screamed, but she was too afraid to move. Who were they coming for tonight? Her? Her siblings? Her parents? What did they want?

As her door opened and she started to scream, figures that seemed nothing more than blurs were grabbing at her, dragging her from her bedroom. They were moving too fast for her to fully comprehend what they were. . .

Suddenly, there were flashing lights. Bright white lights shining on her. She had been stripped of most of her clothing and was strapped to a cold stainless steel table. She could hear the whizzing and buzzing of things around her, though she couldn't see anything yet.

Then there were people around her. Some of them looked human and others had a bluish-silver tint to their skin. Before she had the chance to concentrate on their faces, they were cutting into her.

Gwyn Farrow threw her hand over her mouth to quiet her scream as she sat up in her bed. She was hoping that she hadn't been screaming in her sleep. It would get her into trouble. The doctor would tell her parents, and it could send her back to square one.

She had been in a mental institution for a year now, and she was sick of it. No one believed her story. She supposed that if their positions were reversed, she wouldn't believe her either. It did sound crazy, but if she had wanted to make up a story, she wouldn't have come up with one that had her thrown into an insane asylum. She gained nothing from it.

Gwyn tried to tell her parents that she had been abducted by aliens. She didn't expect them to believe her, but they had listened to her tapes. One night, she had forced herself awake with her heart racing, a sense of fear overwhelming her. The next thing she remembered was waking the next morning. It was strange to her, and she wanted to know what had happened (especially after this had happened several times).

Her siblings began to disappear. . . one by one. At first, people thought it was because the kidnappers expected a very large ransom. The Farrows came from and *were* a very wealthy family. The ransom request never came. Fearing that she would be next and needing a distraction, Gwyn was almost happy to bring her attention back to her night terrors. She placed a voice recorder next to her bed. . . and waited.

Out of the ninety-days she had recorded, thirty of them disturbed her. They all sounded the same. She was protesting and screaming for help. It sounded like she at least *tried* to put up a fight. There was a strange voice, then there was sudden silence. She didn't understand why her parents hadn't heard any of it and she was desperate to show them her tapes. She had been prepared to set up a video recorder when her parents put her into the institution.

She would have understood if she *had* been crazy. They thought she was doing it to get attention because she missed her brothers and sisters. She did miss them. But that had nothing to do with it. Her tapes were real, though she couldn't confirm her theories. She didn't know what had made her remember pieces of her experiences. She thought it might have been the medication.

Her theories were proven right. She was taken shortly after being in the institution. She had no recorders to prove it, but she remembered the experience clearly. Extraterrestrials *did* exist. They *had* abducted her and countless other people. She had seen them on the craft. It explained why her siblings had disappeared. She hadn't seen them there, but she was only in one room. The craft must have been *huge*. They just had to have been there. . . somewhere.

She had been sent home. She returned with the knowledge that some people were sent back and some were not. It made her wonder how they selected who to keep and who to let go. Why did they keep taking the same people? They had taken her repeatedly and she wondered how many of the others she'd seen had been there before. The sad thing was, many of them - if any - wouldn't know what had happened to them.

She was relieved to know that she wasn't crazy, but she was afraid to go to sleep. The abductions only happened at night. When the sun went down, the world seemed so much more frightening now. There was enough craziness in the world without aliens being in it. Why couldn't they bother some other planet? There had to be another place just as interesting to them as Earth. . .

Gwyn wiped her tired eyes and turned on the little lamp next to her bed. She wasn't sure if it had been a dream or if they had abducted her again. She wasn't supposed to have her light on, but it would be off before they noticed anything. Yawning softly, she pulled her mirror out from a drawer. Her dark brown eyes had purple circles under them. She hadn't been sleeping well in the past year. She was hoping that today would change all of that. Her long brown hair was in desperate need of styling. If it all went according to plan, she would be out, get better sleep, and have better hair.

She was about to turn her light back off when there was a flash in the corner of the room. She thought it was the light-bulb of the lamp burning out, but the lamp was fine. She stared into the corner, watching as the figure of a man flickered in her room. What the hell was going on? Was she seeing things? She blinked several times, waiting for the figure to either show itself or disappear. Finally, it disappeared. She shook her head lightly and turned off her lamp. She must have been hallucinating.

Gwyn woke again when it was time to start the day. All she did was sit in her room and wait for her parents to arrive. Today was the day. She was going to go against everything she believed in to go home. She knew that they would believe her. They were just as desperate as she was to have her home. They loved her deeply and she was their only child now. They needed her. . . and she needed to leave this place in order to keep her sanity.

She jumped with excitement when she heard their voices. "Mom! Dad!"

They both looked surprised that she was so thrilled to see them, but she smiled nonetheless. Joseph Farrow was a tall man. His eyes were hazel, and he used to have black hair before the vanishing of his children turned it gray. He was still handsome even though his features were worn.

Katherine Farrow had cut her chestnut brown hair since the last time Gwyn had seen her. Her deep blue eyes were staring curiously at her daughter, anxious to know anything that was new. She sat in one of the chairs near Gwyn's dresser, and Joseph sat in the other. Gwyn paced nervously in front of them.

"How's your painting?" Katherine asked quietly.

"Oh, I haven't been painting lately. I guess I've been. . . thinking."

Joseph shifted in his chair. "What about?"

"I've been thinking that. . . it's time for me to tell the truth." Gwyn stopped her pacing, looking up at them hesitantly. They were waiting for her to continue. "Well, I. . . I made it all up, you see. I was feeling lonely and I. . . wanted attention." Every word made her feel as though she was betraying herself - and she was. "I didn't know what else to do with everything I was feeling. . . acting out seemed like a good idea. . ."

At first, she didn't think they would believe her. Joseph had narrowed his eyes, pondering what she had said, whereas Katherine had already planned her coming home party. "Oh, Gwyn! I'm so happy you've finally admitted it! I want you to come home as soon as you can!"

"Wait just a minute, Kate," Joseph was not as quick to

believe their daughter, "Her doctor needs to tell us if that's possible. *He* needs to say that she's better."

"Well, he will!" Katherine beamed. "You wait and see."

Gwyn barely heard them telling her to wait for them. They were going to make sure that she was well enough to go home. She was so ashamed that she had lied to them. . . it was the only way she could someday tell them the truth.

Her mother was very quick to let her know that she was going to be released. She smiled and jumped around the world; and for some reason, Gwyn couldn't be happy with her. She would be happy when she could prove that she *hadn't* been lying.

She hadn't made any friends in the institute, so there was no need for any goodbyes and well wishes. She just packed what little things she had and tried to get some rest. She had so much on her mind. She had to find her recordings – if her parents hadn't thrown them out. If they *had* thrown them out, she would have to try to make new ones.

If she was lucky, she would be able to capture a video or two as well. They had only taken her once in the asylum and hadn't since. If her recordings were gone. . . how would she continue to prove her theory? What if they stopped coming for her? What if, she could never prove herself right?

Gwyn chewed her lip suddenly very worried and unable to sleep. Her eyes kept looking to the corner to see if the flash had returned. It hadn't. Because she couldn't sleep anyway, she decided to get up and investigate. She ran her fingers along the wall and turned to the window trying to see if a few passing cars could have caused what she thought was the flicker of a man. Then, as she was about to go back to her bed, she heard a voice.

"I'm over here," it said.

She looked to the corner at the opposite side of the room, her jaw dropping as she saw a man standing there. She couldn't scream. She couldn't call for help. The man would probably disappear and the chances of her going home would be slim.

The man had dark wavy brown hair and his eyes were brilliantly blue. Even bluer than her mother's. His cheekbones were very defined, which made him resemble a skeleton in the dark light of the room. "Don't be afraid," he said softly.

What kind of a thing was that to say? How could she *not* be afraid? A stranger was in the room with her. Her door was locked and her window was barred. . . yet. . . he was there with her. *How*? There was only one explanation that she could think of. "You're. . . one of them, aren't you?"

"Yes. . . well, no. . ." he looked confused, as if there was more than one way to answer her question. "I am. . . I used to be. . . I mean, I still am. . . I suppose. . ."

His voice wasn't demonic at all, not like the inhuman voices on her recordings. . . and he *looked* human. Was that the point? Was he trying to trick her? She already knew what he was. . . and he knew that *she* knew. She didn't understand why he looked so different from the others, why his energy *felt* so different. "What do you want?"

He held up one of his hands as a sign of peace, hoping that she wouldn't draw attention to them. He knew that she was going home very soon and she seemed relieved. Of course, he would be relieved to go home too. "I just want to talk to you. I don't want to hurt you."

"I can't trust you," she spoke the words, but she didn't believe them. She wanted to trust him. For whatever reason, her body was telling her to. Was he not a danger to her? Maybe he did really just want to talk. "Please, go. . . I don't understand. . . please leave me alone. . ."

The thing that looked to be a man was not offended by her pleading, but slightly hurt. He hadn't meant to frighten her. He hadn't quite gotten the hang of being around humans yet. He would have to work on that. "I'm very sorry, you must be so scared. . . I promise, I don't mean to harm you. Again, I'm sorry."

Without a beam of light (as she had expected), he disappeared into thin air. What. . . an odd thing to happen. A friendly extraterrestrial. Had they suddenly grown consciences? She was too off-put now to think about it. Sighing softly she climbed into bed and closed her eyes. Her mind kept going over the possibilities of why he had been there. . . and not at all hostile.

***

Gwyn rubbed her arm awkwardly, watching her parents set the last of her boxes on the floor. They had insisted on helping her with anything and everything they could. She wasn't going to refuse their help. She needed to get back into the habit of living again.

"Honey, are you sure about this?" her mother asked as she chewed her lip.

"Yeah," Gwyn nodded, "I'll be fine, mom. I mean, I'm not a baby. I can take care of myself. I know that you guys are worried about me, but I'm going to be fine. I just. . . have to settle in."

Joseph had been scowling from the minute they had picked her up. He didn't think she should be living alone. He was certain that her mind was still fragile. She needed to recover instead of jumping right into things. "Well. . . if something goes wrong, I want you to call us. And I mean something as in *anything*."

Gwyn wanted to say something reassuring to her father. He was a great skeptic and hadn't said very much to her since she'd been committed. She didn't think that was very far. "Yeah. . . okay." That was all she could come up with.

"I don't know about you two, but I'm starving." Katherine smiled happily hoping to take the tension out of the room. "Who's up for Chinese?"

They ate mostly in silence. Joseph was trying to look perplexed by the TV, but the show wasn't about anything that was hard to follow. He was mostly trying not to have a conversation.

On the other hand, Katherine couldn't stop talking. "Oh, sweetie! I forgot to tell you. Your father and I. . . well, we set you up with your very own gallery! We've been telling people about you. We found an agent for you and everything."

"Yeah," Joseph said in a discouraging tone, "Your *mother* appointed herself to the position of your agent."

"Joey, what is so terrible about that? *Really*, I don't see why you're so bothered by it." Katherine finished her plate of food and sank back into her chair.

"Because you don't know anything about it!"

"Well, I thought it would be a nice thing to do with our daughter." She turned to Gwyn, ignoring her husband's negativity. "Does it bother you? I won't be offended if you want someone more. . . experienced."

Gwyn looked between her parents, really wanting to put her father in his place. She didn't want to start a huge fight though. . . not on her first night home. "I think it's great. I just. . . you know. My style of paintings has. . . changed. I hope people aren't expecting sunshine and daises in my work, you know?"

"They don't know what to expect," Katherine said, clearly proud of herself, "I told them that you're unpredictable."

They both knew that Joseph was about to say something derogatory. They were glad when he thought better of it and said nothing at all.

By the time her parents went home, it was late. She had already turned off all the lights, not wanting to unpack everything until tomorrow. No one would care. She was on her own. She wasn't sure what to think about all this space to herself. It was so quiet. . . yet it wasn't peaceful. Knowing what she knew now, she'd never be at peace.

She walked into her bedroom, picking up her most recent paintings and placing them into a spare room. Her parents had all of her older paintings. They were very happy. Full of bright and glorious colors. Her newest paintings weren't so pleasing to the eye.

One or two had a random bit of bright color, but the rest were dark. Blues, black, grays, emerald green, deep purple. . . they were frightening colors in her paintings, and they were meant to be. They hinted at her abduction. . . her experiences. Something about them screamed that they were helpless, afraid, alone. . . just as she had meant for them to. It was exactly how *she* felt.

***

The night of the gallery opening came sooner than Gwyn had wanted it to. Her mother had invited anyone they had ever known, plus strangers and people she thought might make her famous. Gwyn didn't really care about fame. She had so many other things on her mind. Making art for money wouldn't be terrible though.

The only people she knew there were her parents. Everyone there was probably rich. The Farrows had always been very wealthy. Joseph had been born into money. Gwyn didn't really like having money. It meant that she had to socialize with *other* people who had money. Spoiled little rich kids weren't fun to hang around. She had never been one, and that was something she was proud of. Being the youngest, she had seen what being spoiled had done to her siblings; and she didn't want to be snooty.

She watched her mother talking to a circle of people. Everyone seemed happy. She was glad for that. Her mother deserved to enjoy herself even if Gwyn couldn't. Her father had been avoiding her all night and she didn't mind. She didn't feel like talking to him either.

She stopped at one of her more recent paintings. It was hanging beautifully on the wall. The colors on the canvas looked to be even darker because of the lights in the gallery. There was a figure laying on a bed, asleep and two more figures standing in the doorway near the person's bed. She knew what they all symbolized. The poor person who was asleep was colored in blues. The figures in the doorway were gray and black. They were unwelcome.

"What is it?" someone asked.

Gwyn looked to the woman next to her. She was too beautiful to be real. Her hair was long, a dark enough brown to appear black, and it framed her face. Her eyes were an unnaturally piercing green and her lips were ruby red. Where had she come from? "I, uh. . . what do *you* think it is?"

"Oh, I don't know," the woman said in a sing-song voice,

"I think. . . the poor fool is about to be surprised by some very gruesome intruders."

"I think you're right." Much to her own surprise, Gwyn smiled and extended her hand to the woman. "I'm Gwyn Farrow."

"Of course you are," the woman shook her hand, "You're the artist. I'm Anastasia Rothchild. Please, call me Ana. Now that I've seen your work, I guess you could call me a fan."

"I've never had a fan before."

"There's a first for everything." Ana smiled warmly. She was a very friendly person, and Gwyn had the feeling that she wanted to be friends. She had no problem with that. She hadn't had a single friend since she was thirteen. That was before her family started to go missing.

There were many gatherings at the gallery and parties that her parents threw. She was grateful for it even if she wasn't exactly social. To her great relief, Ana showed up to every single one, and she was able to have someone to talk to. They became friends very quickly. It felt so natural. . . almost *too* natural. She supposed she just wasn't used to having a friend. She had to get back into the swing of it.

Gwyn had created a few more paintings. Naturally, her mother had to show them off. She loved the support and being so encouraged, but she didn't know what to say to all the people who came to the parties. They were there to admire and critique her work. What could she say to them without sounding crazy?

She chewed her lip nervously and waved over at Ana, who was talking to a very blonde and very muscular man. He was probably a model. Ana had a knack for attracting men. It was a gift that she had. Gwyn didn't know whether she should be jealous or *glad* that she didn't have that gift. She wouldn't be able to handle men swarming her.

She furrowed her brow now, ceasing the abuse on her lower lip as she felt something. . . familiar. When she turned around, she scouted the room for a face that she knew. She was looking for someone specific. . . someone pretending to be human. She spotted him easily. He was staring right at her.

He walked up to her, the way he moved being so graceful and suave that he *had* to be something supernatural. Though, she had to admit. . . .she had never enjoyed watching someone move so much. It had to be what he was. The attraction had to be unnatural.

"Hello, Gwyn," he said.

"You know my name," she said, not surprised, "I think that's unfair. I'm sure you know everything about me. . . and I know nothing about you."

"There's not much to know." He slowly held out his hand, afraid that she would push it away. "My name is Kael."

"Do you have a last name?" She shook his hand hesitantly.

"Does it matter to you?" When she didn't know how to

answer, he simply chuckled. "It's Manning."

"I would say it's nice to meet you. . ."

"But you hate my guts." Kael nodded.

"I never said that. Don't put words into my mouth." Why had she said that? She *should* hate him. He may not have taken away her family, but he was a part of it. It was more than likely that he had participated in the disappearance of people. So. . . why didn't she hate him?

He wanted to be excited about the fact that she didn't hate him. Somehow, it didn't seem appropriate. "So, uh. . . how are your paintings coming along?"

"They're alright, I guess. I may have underestimated my talent. Either my mother has a magic touch. . . or people seem to like my work." He looked like he wanted to say something. She wasn't sure that she wanted to know what it was. His eyes held so much. . . knowledge. She wanted to know why he looked at her so deeply, so. . . fondly.

"May I see you again?" he asked.

She knew that was coming. "It doesn't really matter if I say no, does it? You'll come around anyway, I imagine." She could have said it cruelly, but she hadn't. For some reason, she found herself *wanting* to see him again.

He must have known this, because he smiled thoughtfully. "Yes. I suppose I will."

Gwyn couldn't let him think that he was getting to her, so

she brushed him off and headed over to her parents. She didn't care who they were talking to or what they were talking about. She just needed a distraction. It already felt as though Kael was inside her, buried beneath her skin and creeping his way into her heart.

Kael was quite proud of himself. Here he had prepared to be laughed at. He had at least expected her to throw something at him. Perhaps she knew what he did. His happy thoughts were ruined when he saw a rather striking brunette across the room.

She nodded for him to follow her, so he did. He followed her into a back room that was dark and empty. He wished it had been a bathroom. He wanted to shove her face into a toilet bowl - preferably one that hadn't been flushed.

She closed the door and smirked at him, her fingers playing with a few strands of her hair. "Hello, Kael."

"What the HELL are you doing here, Ana?"

Ana lost her seductive charm immediately. She didn't appreciate being yelled at by a man who had once been her lover. "I could ask you the same thing, *Kael*. I'm Gwyn's friend. What's your excuse?"

Kael's eyes wandered over the woman's eyes, his face etched with disgust. "You're not her friend. You're just using her."

"What's it to you? I'm still waiting to hear why *you're* at this party. You hate art."

"No I don't. I love art. I only said that to impress you because *you* hated it."

"Awww, Kael," Ana smiled brightly, "I miss those days."

"I don't..." Kael said.

Now she was getting irritated. Why was he treating her this way? "Are you mad at me because I didn't defend you? They were going to banish you either way."

"That was the best thing you ever did, my dear. Being on Earth has led me to my purpose."

"Your purpose?" Ana giggled madly. He was not the man he used to be. "You don't have one, sweet cheeks."

"I couldn't expect *you* to understand. You're too narrow minded." Kael glared at her immensely, hoping that she would take the hint and leave.

"You still haven't answered my question."

If she really wanted to know, he was going to tell her. He was very smug. He knew that she would hate him, maybe enough to stay out of his life. "You know why I'm here." He had intended to sound confident, but he couldn't help the softness in his tone. He was talking about *her*. "I've been searching for her my whole life. Nothing makes sense if I don't feel her existence. I have to be near her to keep a clear head. Even then, she drives me mad. She's everything in me. . . everything that I was meant to be. . ."

Ana narrowed her eyes, trying to think of who he was

describing. It clearly wasn't her. He wouldn't look so content if it had been. . . and that hurt her feelings. "You're not. . . you don't mean. . ."

Kael nodded, more confident now that he had admitted it. "I found her. It took me long enough to find her, but it's the right time. She needs me now. . . just as much as I've needed her since the day I was born."

Ana wanted to vomit on his shoes. Making a mess of his shirt and pants wouldn't be bad either. "How COULD you, Kael?! She is so. . . BENEATH you!"

"I don't care what you think. I don't care what anyone thinks. You must know that by now." He had nothing more to say to her. Giving her another look of repugnance, he walked out of the dark room and was greeted by the bright lights and bustle of the party.

"Hey, we're not finished!" She followed him out, tugging on the back of his shirt to continue their conversation. "There's a way you can redeem yourself. . . you can come home."

Kael sighed impatiently, stopping because she wouldn't rest until she had said what she wanted to say. "I'm not sure I want to go home, Ana. Once upon a time, home was where I longed to be. But things change."

She narrowed her eyes, not knowing what he meant. She remembered when he was banished. He had all but begged them to let him stay. After his first month on Earth, he had cried to her about how alone he felt. "I don't. . .

understand."

"Ana," he said exasperatedly, "I like my life here. I know I wasn't keen on it before, but I'm warming up to people. Besides, I like this look. Human looks good on me, don't you think?"

Now it was *her* turn to be disgusted. "What is *wrong* with you? I *hate* my human form. I hate having a goddamn transmitter embedded in my muscles so that I don't frighten the poor little humans." She gestured to the people around them. "You think they're our equals? We are *so* above them, Kael. We are Godly creatures."

"I used to think that way too," he shrugged, "Honestly, humans are better than us. We may talk like demons and have power they don't possess, but they're better beings."

"How. . . ?" She stared at him, her mouth ajar. "How could you. . . think that?"

"I don't know. I guess I've changed."

"Yeah. . . you have."

Gwyn tilted her head curiously, watching as Kael and Ana had a conversation. She didn't look too pleased with him. He wanted nothing to do with her. So. . . they had met before. Wanting to know what she was missing, she excused herself from her parents and made her way over to the two. "And how do you two know each other? You obviously have a history."

"How could you tell?" Kael asked, rolling his eyes, "Was it

her obvious desire to be a pest or my obvious look of annoyance?"

"We're old friends," Ana said.

"Ah-ha." Gwyn nodded slowly. "Is that why you're following me? You're trying to get close to Ana?" She thought it was a clever observation. Men *always* wanted to be around Ana.

Ana liked this slight accusation. She began to wrap her arm around Kael's waist, and he quickly smacked it away. Without a word to her, he looked at Gwyn. It wasn't her fault that he was in a poor mood now, but she would have to deal with it. "Why is it so hard to believe that I'm interested in *you*?"

He walked away, leaving the two women in awe. They didn't know what to say. Anyone could see that Ana liked Kael. . . and Gwyn liked Kael. Though Kael was only interested in Gwyn. What could she say to her friend? "I, um. . . he keeps showing up."

"Well, stay away from him," Ana said lowly, "He's dangerous."

Gwyn swore that she had seen horns peaking under Ana's dark hair. She probably would have breathed fire if it was humanly possible. "That's funny. . . I don't get a dangerous vibe from him." The funny thing was. . . she was getting the dangerous vibe from *Ana*.

***

Not bothering to knock, Ana walked right into Kael's house. She went up the stairs and straight to his bedroom, her hands on her hips as she stared at him. Her stare was met with his raised eyebrow. He was only in his boxers.

"Did you actually want something, or did you just want to catch me in my bare skin?"

Ana rolled her eyes, though that had been the appealing side of her visit. "Don't flatter yourself."

"It's not like you haven't barged in on me before. . . except I was *completely* bared-skinned then. I was with someone else and very. . . very naked." He turned off his television, knowing that she would stay longer than he wanted her to. "I always seem to be with someone else these days when you see me naked. . . think you could take the hint?"

"You're not with anyone now."

"Yes. . . but I'm not completely naked."

"We could change that."

Kael sighed. "What do you want? The sooner I know, the sooner I can get rid of you."

"You're turning into me, you know. You're stalking Gwyn – like I stalked you."

"Yes, love. I kicked your ass then, and I'll kick your ass now. So get to the point."

"You know it won't last. You're going to ruin it with her."

"No I'm not. I'm going to do everything right. And if she doesn't love me, I'll let her go. Now. . . tell me what you want or I'll throw you out the window." Ana never seemed to understand just how much he hated the sight of her. She had never recovered from the end of their relationship.

Ana reminded herself that she was here for a reason. So, straightening herself up, she looked at him seriously. "We need to talk."

Kael walked into his closet and threw on one of his robes. "Alright. Go on."

She waited for him to reappear from the closet before speaking again. "You can redeem yourself. All of your faults will be forgiven; your past erased. You can start fresh with no judgments and nothing to hold you back."

Of course, his interest was piqued. He had to at least hear what she had to say. No matter how much he liked Earth, he still missed his family. A part of him would always be missing while he was away from them. "How?"

"You have to kill Gwyn."

How could she look at him like that? She looked so relieved, as if it was already settled. "Why does she matter? She's no threat to them."

"You're so wrong." Ana took a step closer to him, her voice almost desperate. "She will destroy us. People will start to listen to her. The humans will start to defend themselves. They'll create weapons to defeat us. If you kill her, you will be a hero. You'll never have to worry about anything again. You will be welcomed with open arms."

He sat down on his bed, letting it all sink in. She had no idea what she was asking him to do. She knew how he felt about Gwyn and she was still asking him to kill her. "I'll. . . have to think about it."

Ana blinked. "But. . . you've been waiting for this chance since you were sent here. . ."

"Goddamn it, I said I would think about it!"

She stood very still, angry because he hadn't agreed to it right away. If thinking would bring him to his senses, she would have to let him. With a low growl, she left his house. Kael shook his head, his head swimming as he rested it in his hands.

The next morning, Gwyn was making breakfast when she sensed something behind her. It would have scared the hell out of her if she didn't know who it was. "Maybe you should knock. . . " She set two plates on the counter, one for him and one for himself.

"You already know who I am. . . *what* I am. Yet you haven't panicked or alerted the public."

"Why would I? They wouldn't believe me. You know that."

He had forgotten that Gwyn didn't know her potential. She didn't know how important she was. "I want. . . I want to have dinner with you. I know that you probably want nothing to do with me, but I want *everything* to do with you."

Well, he wasn't wasting any time. She couldn't deny that she felt something for him. "Why do you appear to be human, and why are you here?"

"I have a transmitter. I've always preferred it to my true appearance. . . and I was. . . a rebel, I guess you could say. They kicked me out."

"Are you a threat to me? To the world?"

Kael shook his head. "No. I still have my abilities, but if I was going to harm you, I would have done it already. And I haven't harmed a human since being here, so. . . will you have dinner with me? Please?"

She had to consider what she was doing. He was the very thing she was trying to fight against. He was her enemy. She was trying to warn the world about his kind. Still. . . she couldn't help herself. "Yes. I will."

Kael lost his balance. She had said yes? They must have been out of their minds. Was that a bad thing? "I. . . don't know what to say. I mean, I haven't. . . been with anyone for years."

"Hey-" she pointed her spatula at him, "-there is no *being* with anyone. We're having dinner. That's all. . . for now."

He smiled. "Understood."

***

Gwyn shifted the bags in her hands, chewing her lip as she watched Ana sip her coffee. They had been silent the entire time they had been shopping. It was so awkward. . . so uncomfortable. Something had changed. Either that, or she was now seeing the true Ana.

She cleared her throat and sat down on an outside bench, wishing she had a coffee of her own as a distraction. "Kael asked me to dinner."

Ana froze. She was grinding her teeth to keep her silence. She couldn't say anything. God, she wanted to. She wanted to make Gwyn feel lost and alone. She wanted to cause her unimaginable pain. . . "What did you say?"

She was hiding something; Gwyn knew it. She couldn't tell Ana anything now. "I. . . said no. It doesn't feel right, you know. . . because he's my own personal stalker. . ."

"Smart girl. I told you he's trouble."

Gwyn sighed softly, closing her eyes in disappointment. She had really wanted Ana to be her friend. Hell, she wanted anyone to be her friend. Ana might have been the only person willing to be. . . and it had to stop.

Gwyn couldn't shake the feeling. There was something very wrong about Ana. . . she was dark. Everything about her was clouded. Gwyn couldn't see into her soul. She couldn't see who her friend was. Now she would never know. She decided right then and there that she didn't want to see Ana anymore.

She was able to put her sadness aside specifically for that

evening. Kael was taking her out tonight. She knew a lot about him simply by being near him. She knew that Kael was special, just as she knew that Ana was evil. She couldn't explain it.

As they sat across from each other at the restaurant, they didn't know what to talk about, but it wasn't awkward. They just kept smiling at each other. Finally, Kael spoke. "Tell me who you are. Tell me about your childhood. . . tell me about your life. I want to know anything you're willing to tell me."

Because of her experience with Ana, she had to be very skeptical of the man sitting across from her because. . . well, he wasn't really a man. "What happens when we're taken? What do the aliens do to humans after they've abducted them?"

Kael was slightly taken aback. He didn't want to tell her out of fear. He didn't want to tell her anything that may jeopardize their relationship. "I. . . well. . . we study you. We. . . operate and experiment. We want to know what *you* are. . . how you work. How much you can endure. . ."

She supposed she shouldn't have asked if she hadn't wanted to hear the truth. Since he had been honest, she could offer him her life. "I had a very happy childhood. I was the youngest. My siblings were very protective of me. Honestly, there's not much to tell. I think my father has always known that I'm different. He's been so cautious, so cold. I think my mother is aware, but she's been the opposite. She loves me as much as anyone can love their child. After my brothers and sisters disappeared. . . they took it hard. They would do anything to keep me. I think that's why they're trying so hard to support me. . . now that they think I'm cured and all."

"Why do you paint?" He tilted his head. "Why do you love it so much?"

She thought for a moment. "When I'm painting I can fly, you know? I can do anything I want. I paint how I see the world. Once brilliant and beautiful., now dark and lonely."

Kael's expression saddened instantly. "I don't want you to think that. The world is still beautiful. Other than you, it's the most beautiful thing I've ever seen. Please don't think it's a horrible place. It isn't. *We* make it seem dark and lonely. I suppose that's the point. But you can't let it get to you. You're so special. . . you're so different. If you don't give people hope, *they* will be lost. The world needs you, Gwyn. More than you know. . ."

Her eyes wandered over him slowly. He was so sweet. . . so sincere. She knew what he was. She could only imagine the things he'd done. Why was *he* so different from *them*? He didn't make her feel alone.

When she was with him, her dark thoughts melted away and the sun came back from its hidden place in her mind. She took his hand in hers, smiling softly at his words. He was trying to give her hope. She wanted to ask about her family, but. . . she didn't want to ruin the way she thought of him. Not yet.

***

Gwyn knocked on the door, waiting for her parents to answer. Her mother greeted her with shaking hands, hurrying her inside and to their living room. Her father was sitting in a chair, staring as though he had been hypnotized. What was wrong with them?

"What's going on?" she asked.

"Oh, Gwyn," her mother said tearfully, "We didn't know you were telling the truth!"

Gwyn furrowed her eyebrows, not understanding at all.

Joseph grudgingly looked up at her, his body sprawled out on the chair. "We've been. . . waking up with this terrible feeling. . . like something bad is about to happen. And that's all we remember. It's suddenly the next day and we're laying in our bed. . . our eyes wide with fright. . . without the slightest idea what happened the night before."

Gwyn's heart sank. Why was her family so important? Why were they all being made to suffer? "I. . . was hoping they would leave you alone. . . it's not like them to make entire families disappear. . ."

"We don't know what to do!" her mother cried. "We're so sorry we didn't believe you before!"

"Mom, it's alright. This may be nothing. . . you may be worried for nothing." She didn't really believe that, but she wasn't going to jump to conclusions without knowing for certain. "Put a voice recorder next to the bed. If something's happening while you're asleep, we'll be able to hear it."

"And what if something *is* happening?" her father asked in a low voice.

"Then. . . we'll deal with it."

Ana stormed off after hearing their conversation. All she had to do was stand outside their house and focus in order to hear them. Once Gwyn discovered that her parents were being abducted too, that would seal the deal. She would plan their destruction.

She was very upset. She needed to see a familiar face, one that wouldn't make her throw up. Naturally, she made herself appear in Kael's house.

Kael wanted to throw the remote across the room when he saw her. "Would you leave me alone? I'm trying to relax and you're not helping."

"Come on, Kael. . ." Ana walked over to him and sat on his lap, an oblivious smirk on her face. "You know you want me."

He pushed her away from him and got to his feet, stepping over to her as he went down the stairs and into his kitchen. Ana followed him.

"What's wrong?"

He opened his refrigerator with great force. "You know what's wrong." Having merely opened it to block his view of her, he closed it. "I'm in love with Gwyn, alright? Get that through your thick skull. Get a tattoo if it'll help you to remember."

Ana stomped her foot, her fists clenched. "Gwyn doesn't know what you've done and she will leave you the minute she does. You're a monster, Kael! She doesn't want to see that side of you; it will disgust her! But *I* love every part of you!"

"I'll tell her about the monster I used to be. . . when I'm ready. Nothing I do in this life concerns you, Ana. It never will. Get out of my house."

After shouting curses for five minutes straight, Ana vanished. Kael took a deep breath to regain his composure before picking up his phone and dialing Gwyn's number. Ana's visits were always taxing on him.

Gwyn was back at home watching a movie when she answered the phone. "Make it quick; the love scene is coming up soon."

His body was still tense, but his face lit up immediately. "It's so good to hear your voice."

She paused her movie, trying not to giggle. "Um. . . how did you get my number?"

"You're not very hard to find. You *are* famous, after all."

She snuggled into the pillows behind her, biting her sleeve anxiously. "Is there a reason you called?"

Kael ran a hand through his hair, clearing his throat

nervously. "Uh, yes. I want to see you again. I feel very mortal at the moment. I think I'm aging. I feel like my life is slipping away and I. . . don't want to waste any time."

Gwyn scratched a torn part of her jeans, not wanting to tell him that she was eager to see him as well. "I'm doing a talk show later today. You can meet me there."

With a grin, he accepted and got the information from her.

Gwyn was later sitting on a couch next to the interviewer, thinking that she should have been shaking with nervousness. She wasn't, though. It was as if this was what she was supposed to be doing. . . it was natural.

The woman next to her was a few years older than her. Her hair was long and black and her eyes were brilliantly green. She had very trusting features. "So, Gwyn. . . you claim that something has repeatedly taken you from your home. They're intruders, but they're not human. What exactly are they?"

"Well, it is my firm belief that they are not from this planet," she said confidently.

"You think they're extraterrestrials?"

"I do."

"I don't think you can blame us for questioning your sanity."

"No, not at all. In fact, my parents did. I was in a mental institution for a while. Oddly enough, that was where I had the first abduction experience that I can remember."

"So. . . your theory is that aliens abducted you."

"Oh, not just me. My whole family, actually." Gwyn thought she was lucky so far. No one was laughing at her.

"Do you have any proof?"

"Not yet. Once I do, I promise you that I'll share it with the world."

The host nodded slowly, examining her before continuing with the interview. "You know what? I believe you, Gwyn. It's such a frightening thought, which is why most people refuse to accept it."

"I know it is. Believe me, I'm still afraid. But I'm not the only one with this theory. There are so many people who have come forward. And they're usually laughed at."

"We know that all of your siblings have gone missing. What do you think happened to them?"

"I don't think. . . I know." It was difficult for her not to get emotional at this point, but she needed to finish the interview. "They were taken, same as me. They just didn't get to come back home."

The woman shook her head. "Knowing what's happening all over the world. . . having lost your family and experienced being abducted yourself. . . how can you move on with your life?"

Gwyn smiled warmly, looking over to Kael in the audience. She looked away before it brought attention to him. "We don't have to stop living our lives. We can't let them take that away from us. I won't let them have that power over me." The audience was soaking up every word. "We can beat this together. . . all of us. I mean, how do people deal with war? This *is* a war. . . and we *will* fight it."

As soon as the host clapped, the audience did too. It was astounding to her. It wasn't long ago that she thought she would always be alone in the world. But these people believed her. . . and that was a start.

Kael beamed at her. He was so proud. They loved her for who she was; she was so honest and gentle. He had to admire her. It was bound to become a habit.

Gwyn was still grinning from ear to ear when they sat to dinner. It was a contagious grin, but his cheeks were hurting. Hoping she would say something, he raised his eyebrows at her.

She giggled and took her hand across her mouth, forcing her lips to stop grinning. "So. . . tell me about *your* life. What was your childhood like? What are your people like? Are you immortal?"

"We're a lot like humans, actually. Instead of presidents, we have royal families. Um. . . we eat food that's similar to yours. We all have jobs. . . we eat. . . sleep. . . shit. . . and reproduce."

"Please say something else to wash away the image of you

shitting."

Kael laughed softly. "Some of us prefer to have our transmitters at all times. I do. It also helps our scientists to appear human when they. . . experiment. In case a patient catches a glimpse of them."

Gwyn nodded. "Very clever. So. . . the immortal thing?"

"We're not immortal. We live around three hundred years, as long we don't fall ill or. . . we're not killed."

"You can be killed? You can get sick?"

"Oh, yes. But the weapons aren't like yours. Bullets can hurt a lot, but they won't kill us. Fire will. . . blasts of energy will. . . and the metal would have to be the strongest in the world to penetrate our skin. We have diseases like yours. . . only they're stronger. If humans were to catch them, they would be dead within days."

"Wow." Gwyn blinked, taking in all of this fabulous information. He must have known that she would use it to her advantage. "So, uh. . . three hundred years? I'll be dead long before you."

Kael closed his eyes and shook his head lightly. She watched him as his eyes reopened and he held her hand across the table. "Please don't say that. It's. . . painful to think that you could die. . . that you *will* die. I've never felt like this before and I don't understand it. I don't understand all these intense feelings."

Gwyn rubbed over the back of his hand with her thumb.

"You feel for me the way I feel for you."

He smiled happily giving her hand a gentle squeeze. How she could love him. . . he didn't know. He didn't want to.

"So, how old are you now? How will you age?"

"I'm one hundred and two years old. We age the way you do, just. . . much more slowly. I think being here changes the rules. I have wrinkles around my eyes when I smile."

"I know you do. I like them, though. They make you seem more human."

"Would you prefer that I was a man?"

She shrugged. "If it would change who you are now. . . no."

When they were finished with dinner, they went back to Gwyn's house. Hours had passed, and all they did was lay in her bed in each other's arms. She was about to fall asleep when he nuzzled her forehead.

"Gwyn. . . do you feel guilty about being with me?"

She looked at him sleepily, her hand on his chest. "No. I know that you're different from the others."

He was quiet for a minute, but continued before she fell asleep. "Do you hate them? My people, I mean."

Gwyn shook her head, wondering why he wanted to have such a serious conversation as she was drifting off. "I want nothing more than to have peace between my world and yours."

Kael couldn't stand it any longer. He didn't care if her memory gave out and she forgot it in the morning. Slowly and gently, he pressed his lips to hers. She was awake enough to respond and touch his cheek. Then, unable to keep them open, she closed her eyes. He smiled softly, still holding her as they fell asleep.

***

It had been a month since she had told her parents to record themselves sleeping. They were sitting nervously in the living room. Gwyn hadn't wanted Kael to come along, but he had insisted. He said that he might be able to help. She was grateful. She just didn't want to tell her parents what he was. That could wait.

Katherine had made tea and tried to impress Kael with Gwyn's many attributes. There was no need. He was already in love with her. He wondered if he would ever be able to tell them that.

When silence fell over them, Gwyn pressed play and they sat, listening to the sound of Katherine and Joseph's steady breathing. Out of the four of them Kael was the most uncomfortable. He was holding Gwyn's hand tightly, hoping that they wouldn't hear anything to cause alarm.

The breathing became heavier. Then Joseph yelled something, trying to wake his wife. There was the sound of something else in the room. As it spoke, Kael listened intently, trying to hear what it was saying. It wasn't good. After what sounded like Joseph trying to fight off the intruder, there was silence.

Gwyn stopped the tape. They didn't need to hear any more. "I wish I could tell you that I tampered with the recordings. . ."

"You were right all along, then?" Joseph asked dully, "I had you committed for telling the truth. . . for trying to warn us?"

Kael shifted slightly, looking over at Gwyn, who was very calm. "Dad, I don't blame you. Now that we know this is happening to you two. . . well. . . you're aware of what's happening."

Katherine wiped away quite a few tears before she was able to talk. "Wh-what can we do, Gwyn?"

"We have to get people's attention. We have to let as many people know as we can. We'll start out with our country. . . and perhaps, if it's bad enough, we'll tell the world."

Kael was staring at the floor. He wanted to offer his opinion and advice, but he couldn't. Not in front of her parents. How could she not care what he was? She must have, at least a little. If she didn't. . . she wouldn't avoid asking what he did before coming to Earth.

"Gwyn," Joseph said slowly, "Is this what happened to our family? They were. . . abducted? These aliens. . . or whatever they are. . . they took your brothers and sisters?"

She couldn't say anything; she only nodded. She had to control her emotions and not cry in front of them. They would be sad enough on their own.

Sure enough, Katherine started to sob uncontrollably. Joseph rushed to comfort her, his arms around her tightly as he avoided the eyes of his daughter and her apparent boyfriend.

Gwyn stood up and Kael did with her, still holding her hand. "I'm going to leave you alone. I know you need time to grieve. I'll be back soon, alright?"

Joseph nodded solemnly. Katherine said nothing.

Gwyn sighed and took Kael outside. She knew that she had understood the tape more than her parents had. "What was said? That voice. . . it was one of your kind, wasn't it?"

"Yes," Kael said hesitantly, "But that's all you need to know. You just had a very emotional experience. I don't want to make you feel any worse. Why don't you go home and get some rest?"

"I've already cried for my family," she said, "I'm done crying. I want to fight for them. I want to stop this from happening to other people. Tell me what it said."

Kael let go of her hand, his heart aching. He knew she would feel terrible about it. "It was a male. . . and he said that. . . your father wouldn't be able to protect himself or your mother. He said that they have *you* to blame. . . for what will be done to them."

Gwyn still didn't understand why the aliens were so set against her. She had never done anything to them. She wrapped her arms around herself, now feeling very cold. "Oh. Well. . . I think I'm going to take your advice. I'm feeling a little tired. Can we talk later?"

"Yeah, of course." Kael kissed her forehead. It hurt him to feel her sadness. "Call me when you need me."

She gave him a disheartened smile, and then walked off.

Kael wanted to throw something. He wanted to tear down a house and punch through brick walls. He couldn't take away her pain. He would never be able to make up for what his kind hand done to hers. It was impossible not to think that she would resent him. Someday. . . soon. . . she would start to hate him. He couldn't stand that.

He walked home and threw himself onto his bed, closing his eyes to get rid of the images that were flashing before them. It didn't help. When he heard Ana's footsteps, he wanted to throw her somewhere very far away.

"Have you made a decision yet?" she asked in a cheerful tone.

Kael opened his eyes and hopped off his bed, preparing himself for her wrath. "Yes, I have."

Ana clapped her hands excitedly, smiling brightly. "I hope you made the right one."

"I did. I'm not going to do it."

Her smile left instantly. Ana's fists clenched and unclenched, tempted to hash out their feelings then and there. "I thought we were going to be together. If you would just kill the bitch and come home, we *could* be together! I can make you happy!"

"SHE makes me happy, Ana. You never did. I love Gwyn and it eats you up inside, doesn't it? You know that I never felt anything for you that comes *close* to what I feel for her." Kael stormed passed her, trotting down the stairs and knowing that she was right on his heels.

"Your parents! Your sister! They're going to be heartbroken!"

He stopped and turned to face her at the bottom of the stairs, his anger boiling beneath his skin. "They don't know the meaning of the word."

"Oh, and *you* do?!"

"It's what I'll be without Gwyn." He wished that he could threaten *her* in some way. It was really a threat to his parents. "You tell them. . . they had better let me have this."

"Don't you worry. I'll tell them that their son is a traitor. In love with a human. . . the shame!" Ana would have kicked him across the room if she hadn't known better. Instead, she punched him as hard as she could.

He watched her disappear, screaming angrily as he threw his fist into his wall. Miraculously, he managed not to collapse the house.

He waited a few days to let himself cool off. Then he went to Gwyn's house, barging in unannounced. It wasn't the brightest thing to do. He just. . . he had to know.

Gwyn looked up from a stack of papers she had been looking over. Nothing was more important than whatever Kael felt he needed to say. "Is something wrong?

Kael steadied his breathing, his fists clenched, though his anger wasn't at all directed at her. "Are you afraid of me?"

She was confused as to why he was so angry. She hadn't thought the event at her parents' house had affected him. "No. . . I'm not."

"Are you sure about that? I mean, I know almost everything about you simply by looking at you. You don't know who I am. You don't know who I was. You don't. . . you don't know the terrible things I've done."

Gwyn shook her head, abandoning her stack of papers and taking his hands in hers. "I don't want to know. I should be afraid. . . I know that. Here I am, thinking of ways to defeat aliens and. . . you're one of them. I don't even know how that makes you feel."

"To hell with them," he said, his voice nearly breaking, "I don't care. You're all I want. I'll be by your side, no matter what happens. I'll help you in any way I can."

This was a great comfort to her. She smiled softly and nodded as she gently squeezed his hands. "I'm so relieved. I need your help, actually. The military has contacted me. So has the president. They want to start preparing for a war. They want people to be able to defend themselves. The details that you gave me were very vague. If you could work with us to design weapons. . . we won't have to reveal who you are. We could make up some bogus story to explain how you know everything. I would. . . really appreciate your help."

He was going to help Gwyn and her country learn how to kill his species of extraterrestrials. Somehow, he didn't feel obligated to protect his people in any way. The love of his life was his priority and if she needed his help, he would give it to her. "Of course I'll help you. Whatever you need."

It may have been unfair of her to ask him such a thing, but she assumed he would say something if it bothered him. With a happy sigh, she smiled and wrapped her arms around him.

***

Gwyn had been on numerous talk shows. Articles were written about her. People wanted to know the truth. They had begun to work with the military to create weapons that would harm and kill aliens. It was going well. It made Kael nervous to be around so many people who didn't know that he was the very thing they wanted to kill. Other than that, he didn't mind helping.

Gwyn was relieved to finally be doing something. She was helping. With Kael beside her she was confident that they would be able to win a war - if there was one. They weren't helpless anymore. That was what mattered.

Kael stroked Gwyn's hair as they snuggled in her bed, trying to figure out how to put his question subtly. There wasn't a way that he could. He knew that *she* knew something was bothering them and it was making them both uneasy. So, deciding it was time he said something, he took a deep breath. "Gwyn, these weapons that we're making. . ."

She looked up at him, waiting for him to continue before assuming his thought process. "Yes?"

"Well. . . you can imagine my fear, can't you? I have to wonder if these weapons will ever be used. . . on *me*."

She didn't want to think about that. What if someone *did* find out about him? "I would never do that. I could never hurt you, Kael. I guess. . . it is possible that someone will find out eventually. . . but you know me. I wouldn't use the weapons against *you*. And it's alright if you're worried about your family. I'm worried about mine. I know that loving me doesn't change what you feel for your kin."

"My kin. . ." Kael shook his head. "I'm ashamed to call them that. I mean, I *feel* human. I don't feel like I'm one of them. I feel like I'm the same as you. . . like we're equals." He shook his head again, quickly this time. "Wait. You said. . . does this mean you know that I love you, then?"

Gwyn giggled, hitting his chest playfully. "I've known since the day we met. And I want you to know that the feeling is mutual."

He could only describe it as pure bliss. He didn't care

about his family in this moment. He didn't care about Ana, he didn't care about the war, he didn't care that they could both be dead within a year. None of it mattered. . . none of it. *She loved him.* "I have to say that I've doubted-"

Gwyn shut him up with a kiss. It was gentle and sweet. . . and that was how they kept it. They didn't want to tempt themselves into going any further. It wasn't the right moment. They would know when it was.

***

"What the hell is this?" Kael held up a bag of cotton candy, his face twisted in disgust. It was pink and baby blue, colors that didn't look good on a giant ball of cotton.

Gwyn laughed as she took it from him. She opened the bag and tore off some of the blue candy. When she tried to put it in his mouth, he backed away. "It's called cotton candy."

"Okay. . . what *is it?*"

"Oh, it's just sugar. . . spun really fast. . . and dyed different colors."

"Gwyn, you're going to rot your teeth. I don't know how you can eat this crap and you will never get me to taste it."

"You're no fun!" She whacked his shoulder and placed the cotton candy on her tongue, letting him watch as it melted there.

He cleared his throat and started to walk with her keeping

in mind how cold it was. Why there was a fair in February – he didn't know. It wasn't snowing, but that was no excuse. He didn't understand how people could have so much fun when they could see their own breath. "I thought we were going to behave for as long as we could."

Gwyn shrugged, smiling and waving when she saw her parents. "I don't know how much longer I'll be able to behave. It's extremely cold, yet. . . I feel very hot."

"News flash. You *are* hot." Kael hid a smirk as they stopped at her parents.

Katherine and Joseph both gave small smiles and no one knew what to say. It was annoying all of them.

"Um. . . let's have dinner soon," Gwyn suggested.

"I'd like that." Katherine tried to smile in a friendly way towards Kale, but her husband's obvious disapproval faltered it.

"Well, enjoy your evening." He knew it was rude. They were making Gwyn feel uncomfortable and he didn't like it, so he took her arm and walked away from her parents.

Gwyn knew it was rude too, but she couldn't help laughing. "You're so sweet. . . I think you just proved my father right, though."

"Oh, I don't give a damn if they like me or not. As long as you do, their opinion means very little to me."

"Hey," Gwyn tore off a piece of pink cotton candy, "I

don't like you. I *love* you."

Kael stopped walking. "I may just love you more. . ."

"Oh. . . shut up and eat some candy."

He avoided her hand as much as he could. Finally, she was able to force the cotton candy into his mouth. He stood there with his mouth open, not sure what to make of it. Gwyn tore off another piece and put it in her own mouth, then touched her tongue with his before letting their lips touch.

Kael smiled, his entire body tingling. He wanted to blame it on the sugar. They both knew what it was. "I think I like cotton candy. . ."

Gwyn ran her fingers through his hair, smiling happily as she made it untidy. "I thought you would."

He had to force himself to look away from her, the sense of danger overwhelming him. When he saw Ana standing a few feet behind Gwyn, his heart started to race. "What do you want?"

"I just wanted to see the happy couple." Ana smirked at him. She was so calm, and that was unlike her. Ana always had extremely high energy. It didn't matter what she did. Her calmness was throwing him off.

He narrowed his eyes at her. He needed to see what was going on behind those satisfied eyes. . . she knew something he didn't. That must have been it. "We *are* happy. So leave us be."

Ana giggled in a mad way that only *she* could. "You're jumping to conclusions. Do you honestly think that I would end you in public?"

Kael released Gwyn and strode furiously to Ana, his hand gripping her arm so violently that it gave her almost instantaneous bruises. "If you lay one finger on her, so help me God. . . I will end *you*."

Ana merely grinned. She was far too collected for his liking. "When I kill her. . . I'll use more than one finger, my sweet."

Kael growled furiously, and he was attracting attention. Gwyn put her hand on his shoulder hoping it would calm him.

She was shaking like a leaf. It was embarrassing. To hear Ana threaten her life. . . it was unnerving. She didn't know why. Ana may have been in love with Kael, but that was no reason to threaten anyone. "Kael. . . you can't do this here."

Feeling the shaking hand on his shoulder, he grudgingly let Ana go. He gave her one last spiteful glare, then put his arm around Gwyn's shoulder. "Come on. Let's get you home."

She didn't argue. Gwyn expected Ana to follow them, but she didn't.

It was difficult for her to fall asleep that night. Kael had to calm her down with tea and a chick flick. He forced laughs at the lame jokes and tried to look teary-eyed when the scene was supposed to be moving. It cheered her up.

He didn't know what was going on. He couldn't see any of his surroundings. It was all a blur. He could hear two voices. . . he knew both of them. He followed the voices until he found who was talking.

Gwyn and Ana were having a very heated discussion. He wanted to run to them and stop them before something bad happened, but he was too late. Ana grinned at him, her hand held out in front of her. There was a blast of blue light. . . then nothing. Darkness.

He waited for the blurs to return. When they did, he searched frantically for Gwyn. Why couldn't he find her? Had Ana sent her to another planet? Had his one true love been obliterated?

"Gwyn! Gwyn, where are you? Say something, please?"

Then he saw her. She was sprawled out in front of him, her empty eyes staring at his shoes. Her chest and stomach were covered with blood. She wasn't moving. . . she wasn't breathing.

Out of the corner of his eye, he saw Ana cackling, blending in with the rest of the blurs. He was left alone with Gwyn's body; Ana's laughter was the only sound he could hear.

"No!" Kael panted heavily as he sat up in Gwyn's bed. She was sleeping soundly beside him. Careful not to wake her, he quietly got out of the bed and made his way down into the kitchen.

It was only natural that he should have a dream like that. Ana had threatened Gwyn's life that night. He couldn't blink away the image of her lifeless eyes. . . if that dream ever came true, it would be his fault.

It didn't take Gwyn long to see that he wasn't in the bed with her. If he was going to be awake, she wanted to be awake with him. She dragged herself out of bed and went down to the kitchen. He was splashing water onto his face.

"Kael?"

He turned off the faucet, sighing as he saw her. She was absolutely perfect. Her pink nightgown matched the color of the cotton candy they had eaten earlier. "I'm sorry, did I wake you?"

"Not directly, no." She took a step closer to him. "Are you okay?"

Kael shook his head, wiping the water from his face. "The look in Ana's eyes tonight. . . I had a nightmare. I can't be in a world that doesn't have you in it."

"Well. . . you can just go back to *your* world, can't you?" She knew it was a terrible joke and she shouldn't have said it. He was clearly shaken by whatever had happened in this dream. She could only guess.

"Don't do that. I'm serious, Gwyn. You don't know how your existence has changed me."

"I don't know because you won't tell me. I want to know who you are, Kael. But you insist on hiding your life from me. I don't think it's fair."

He shook his head again. "You're right. It isn't. But I'm not ready to lose you. I don't. . . I don't want to become a monster again."

"If you want me to understand, you're going to have to tell me something about yourself."

Kael rubbed the back of his neck, hesitant to say anything at all. He didn't know what he would say; something he wanted her to know? Something he didn't? "Ana. . . and I – we used to be involved."

Gwyn would have laughed if Ana was anyone other than who she was. If they were all normal people in a completely normal situation, it might be something to laugh about. "You were. . . involved?"

"We were, you know. . . together. A couple. . . lovers. . ."

"I know what you meant." She didn't care what they were in the past, as long as things really *had* changed. "Were you in love?"

"I thought it was love. It wasn't. *She* loved *me*. She still does."

"I know that. She doesn't try to hide it."

"Yeah, well. . . she's like me. She's an alien. We were *not* good people, Gwyn. . . and she hasn't changed like I have."

Gwyn put her hands on his shoulders. This meant nothing to her. "As long as *you've* changed, I couldn't care less about Ana."

"You don't understand," he said desperately, "She's as evil as they come. I had a dream that she killed you. I couldn't see you. . . I couldn't find you. . . I couldn't. . . *save* you."

"Oooh. . . " She sighed, finally realizing why he was so upset. "That's what this is about."

Kael blinked back the tears in his eyes, his voice becoming more distressed with each word. "I would do anything to protect you. I just know that I can't protect you from her. . . not if she's determined to keep us apart."

"Hey," she put her hands on both of his cheeks, forcing him to look into her eyes, "Nothing can keep us apart. Not even death."

He just stared at her. She wasn't fazed by this information. She wasn't nearly as afraid for her life as he was. "How can you do that? How can you be so strong?"

"Because you are my strength." She kissed him gently, her grip on his shoulders tightening. This was it. . . she could feel it.

Kael felt as if all his energy had been building up inside him, just waiting for this moment. He picked her up and carried her back up the stairs. Her heart was racing with anticipation as he set her carefully on the bed.

She had never been so nervous in her life. She wasn't a virgin, though she could count how many times she had had sex on one hand. But this was different. They weren't going to have sex; they were going to make love. . . and she had never done that before.

He was as nervous as she was. Ana was the only woman he

had ever been with, and their time together had been anything *but* loving. It was rough and angry. This was something *he* had never done before. He didn't know what the hell he was doing. But he would not – under *any* circumstances – be with Gwyn the way he had been with Ana.

Gwyn knew that one of them had to do something. Kael was frozen with fear just as she was. She forced herself to pull off his shirt, chewing her lip out of nervous habit. He slipped off her nightgown very *slowly*, knowing that she was uneasy too. He wanted to give her time to stop him.

She smiled apprehensively, kissing his shoulder as she got on her knees to pull off his jeans. Her nightgown fell away and she tossed it to the floor. His breathing was unsteady as he took in her appearance, his hands slowly sliding off her panties. She was embarrassed that she was so anxious to be naked in front of him for the first time. She was glad that she was finally undressed. The pressure was off.

He almost stopped her from pulling off his boxers, then he remembered that it was necessary for what they were about to do. It was a relief to feel her tension. At least he wasn't the only one who was terrified.

Gwyn laid back into the pillows on the bed, waiting for him to be ready to join her. After taking a few deep breaths, he stepped out of his boxers and climbed onto the bed. His body hovered above hers for a moment before he let their bodies press against each other.

Kael kissed her softly, placing himself at her opening and

entering her with a gentle thrust. When she gasped, he took it as a bad sign. She just smiled at him. "It's okay," she whispered.

Her eyes closed as he pushed himself deeper. Now that he was here, above her and watching her extraordinary face, it didn't seem so awkward. It was. . . right. This was where he belonged. He had always thought it, but now he *knew* it.

He smiled warmly, trailing kisses from the very top of her neck down to her left breast. She sighed in pure delight as she felt him moving inside of her. She had never imagined that it would be this perfect, though she *had* hoped.

Their breathing was heavy, but they were both completely relaxed. The sound of her breathing, the sound of her heart beating. . . it was the most beautiful sound in the world to Kael. It was very calming.

He pushed himself as deeply inside of her as her body would allow. The feeling was incredible. Each movement issued a soft groan from his lips. Gwyn wrapped her arms around his neck, her eyes shut tightly as beads of sweat formed on her forehead.

His thrusting was slow, and with each new thrust, she would let out a small breath. The sound was exciting to him, more so than her moans. Her breathing was still soothing, even if it *was* elevated.

Kael pulled her hands up and placed them on both sides of the pillow before he entwined his own fingers with hers. She wanted to express her happiness in this moment, but grinning and giggling like an idiot didn't seem appropriate. Instead, she bit her bottom lip, knowing that she wouldn't last much longer.

He kissed her passionately, squeezing her hands. She squeezed them back as she released. Kael came just after she did, and they were both completely out of breath. He remained on top of her for a while, letting them feel each other. There was no other way that they could be so close to each other. Now having felt such a connection, he wanted to cherish every second until it happened again.

Gwyn let out a slow breath, finally being able to breathe normally again. She nuzzled his cheek with hers and he smiled. It was highly contagious. He gently removed himself from her and laid beside her on the bed, staring at the designs on the ceiling as if they were the stars. He was lost in feeling.

"Kael?"

He looked over at her, trying to snap himself out of it. "Yes?"

"I'm a little cold. . ."

Kael chuckled quietly and pulled the sheets over their bodies, then wrapped his arms around her. "Better?"

She nodded as she snuggled against his chest. "Much better."

He continued to stare at the ceiling, his mind void of thought for the very first time in his life. What was this?

How could he describe it? It was so much more than happiness.

Although Gwyn wanted nothing more than to wallow in the blissful silence, her doubts were getting the better of her. "Kael. . . are you keeping something from me?" She knew that he was. She hated to ruin the moment, but she had to question him at a time like this.

She could have asked so many other questions that he would have answered, and she had to ask what he was trying to put out of his mind. "Yes."

"Are you going to tell me what it is?" She didn't want them to have secrets from each other. She knew that it must have been shameful. Still, she knew that she would get past it.

He wanted to tell her everything. He didn't *want* to keep anything from her, especially not now. She wasn't ready. *He* wasn't ready. He couldn't bring himself to say that he had tortured people; that he had killed them. She didn't need to hear that yet. "Not tonight, my love."

She hadn't really expected him to reveal his secrets. It was worth a try. Tightening her arms around him, she fell asleep. Kael stayed awake for hours, his mind no longer calm. It was spinning.

***

Kael had been wandering through Gwyn's house as she prepared dinner. She said that she didn't want him stealing samples, so he was sent away. He was distracting himself by looking through her journals and photo albums.

There was so much in her life that he had missed. He knew that it had all happened, but it didn't seem real to him because he hadn't been there. There was a point when pictures of her had stopped being taken and her journals were left with pages yet to be filled. The most recent pictures and information about her was all over the news. People were raving about her. . . they trusted her.

He suddenly had the urge to rip all the pictures to pieces and burn the pages in her journals. Until his kind had come along, her life had been something of a fairytale. She had a family. She had hopes and dreams. She reached for the stars and wanted all that the world had to offer. She was still the same. . . but the knowledge of life beyond Earth had changed her. She was frightened.

"Why are you so upset?" Kael turned around to find his little sister. She hadn't gotten any taller. She always wore heels to hide how short she really was. She was dressed in human clothing. Her brown hair was to her shoulders, shorter than the last time he had seen it. Her chocolate brown eyes were staring at him. . . searching.

"It's just. . . her memories. . . her life. None of them are mine. They don't *deserve* to be mine. *We* did this to her, Liza."

Liza hugged her brother quickly, then stood back and

looked at him again. "I'm jealous, you know. We grew up believing that this love was impossible. It was a dream. But it's your reality. . . and you two are very lucky."

Shaking his head, Kael shoved a photo album where it belonged on its self. "I know we are. I always knew it was possible. I was just afraid of it and I did so many things to avoid it finding me. And it found me anyway."

"I wish I could tell you that you don't have to be afraid anymore. . ."

He knew that there was so many other things that he had to worry about. Being with Gwyn complicated everything. It was all easier without her in his life. . . but it wasn't *better.*

"Do you know what's happening?"

"America is preparing for war."

"It could be worse. It could be the whole *world.*"

"I know. . . we're preparing anyway."

That wasn't something he wanted to hear. Humans were only preparing in *case* a war should come. Now it was inevitable. "I don't want there to be a war. I don't want to fight."

"Only our parents are participating. Our sector is the going to be the only one fighting. A country against a country. That's fair, isn't it?" Liza was innocent. She didn't want to see the evil in *any* world, and she wasn't going to alarm herself if there was no cause for it. Until something dreadful happened, she would keep a cool head and see both sides.

"I suppose it is. . . seeing as I've helped to create weapons that can harm us. . ." He avoided her gaze guiltily.

"I'm not angry at you, Kael; mother and father are. I know what this world means to you. And I will try to make them see your side of things."

"Kael!" Gwyn called from downstairs.

Liza took this as her cue to leave. "Keep your chin up. I'll see you soon."

Gwyn found him in the small room she used for storage, her smile so bright that it was blinding. "Come on, you! They're here."

He followed her grudgingly down the stairs. He didn't want to have dinner with her parents. They didn't like him, and it made a peaceful dinner very difficult. They would probably make up an excuse to leave early. If it wouldn't disappoint Gwyn, he would be glad for it.

They were silent during the meal, except for the occasional asking for the bread or vegetables to be passed. Even if the TV was on, it would take the elephant out of the room.

Joseph was his usual self. He only looked at Gwyn and Kael if he absolutely had to. And Katherine couldn't *stop* looking at them. Kael knew that they were both burning to say something, so he spoke up. "What is it?"

Katherine looked worriedly at her husband, clutching her fork for dear life. "We. . . we want to know. . . I mean to say, we know that. . ."

Joseph asked the question that his wife couldn't bring herself to. "What are you, Kael? We know you're not human. Not a normal one, at least."

Gwyn pushed her plate of food aside, her eyes focused on Kael. "It's not my secret to tell."

Kael didn't see the point in keeping it from them, although it could be very dangerous to reveal it to her father. He wasn't exactly friendly. "Well. . . I'm. . . not from Earth. I'm an alien. An alien prince, actually."

"Is that supposed to mean something to us?" Joseph said, his voice steadily rising, "Who gives a damn if you're royal on your planet?! You're a fucking extraterrestrial and you're HERE with MY DAUGHTER!"

Gwyn wanted to throw herself in front of Kael to protect him from her father. "Daddy, calm down. I'm in love with him. That's not *his* fault."

Katherine tried to touch Joseph's arm to comfort him, but he pushed it away. "I want to know. Where you come from. . . your. . . *kind*. Are they the ones who have been terrorizing my family?"

Kael held his breath, knowing that his response would be answered with an extreme burst of anger. "Yes."

Sure enough, Joseph tackled him to the floor. "YOU

RUINED MY FAMILY!"

Kael could crush him easily, but he wasn't going to touch Gwyn's father. *He* would heal; her father wouldn't. "I know. . . I'm sorry."

"Get away from him!" Gwyn got up from the table, and watched her father as he attempted to squeeze the life out of Kael.

"YOU STAY AWAY FROM MY DAUGHTER! DO YOU HEAR ME?!" Joseph squeezed Kael's throat expecting his face to turn pale or at least a pained shade of red.

Kael needed to breathe, but Joseph wasn't hurting Kael nearly as much as he was hoping to be. "I'm not forcing her to be with me." It was important for him to remain calm when the man above him was losing his mind.

"Dad, leave him alone!" Gwyn pulled on her father trying to get him away from Kael.

"YOU!" Joseph launched himself at his daughter and shook her violently. "HOW COULD YOU BE WITH HIM?! YOU CRIED TO US ABOUT HOW HORRIBLE THESE CREATURES WERE, AND NOW YOU'RE FUCKING ONE OF THEM?!"

"That's enough!" Kael could have used enough force to crush Joseph into dust, but he only threw the man away from Gwyn.

Katherine was still at the table sobbing hysterically into her hands. Joseph allowed himself to collect his breath, then he grabbed Katherine by the arm and pulled her out of the house with him.

Gwyn was standing in the middle of the kitchen shaking as she tried to absorb what had happened. Her father's eyes were worse than Ana's had been. Kael didn't know what to say that would help her. "I'm sorry, Gwyn. I didn't mind when he went after me, but I couldn't let him hurt you."

He was waiting for her to scream at him-to blame him as her parents did. Instead of getting angry and making them both feel worse, she threw her arms around him and cried into his chest. He sighed sadly and held her gently; he wished he could take away her pain. That was the one ability he didn't possess.

After she was finished crying, she dried her tears; she kissed him deeply knowing that being close to him would make her feel better. He kissed her back; his hands gripped her sides as they gradually found their way to the kitchen floor.

***

Months had passed. Gwyn's parents refused to speak to her. Katherine still helped her with the gallery and showed up to whatever talk show where Gwyn was guest appearing. It was better than seeing neither of her parents. Her father had never been a very loving man anyway. She didn't know how many times her father had actually said 'I love you' to her mother. . . once. . . twice. . . ? Gwyn considered herself lucky; she had Kael.

She was preparing the country for war. It was nice to have support from *someone*. Without Kael, she wouldn't have anyone at all. People thought that she had hundreds of friends and plenty of family to cling to in these troubled times. They were so wrong. She had *no* friends. All she had left was Kael. Her parents may still have been alive, but she knew that she was dead to her father. It wouldn't be long before her mother turned on her too.

Gwyn was looking over designs for new weapons in the kitchen. They had to be ready. Even Kael insisted that they make as many weapons as possible as *fast* as possible. He didn't want them to be caught unprepared. He was worried about Gwyn. He was only worried about the rest of the country because he knew that she would blame herself for anything that happened to them.

He brought her a glass of water, picked up the designs, and put them in the living room. "That's enough for now, don't you think? You don't have to memorize what they look like. You just have to know what they do and how to use them."

"I know, I know," she sighed exasperatedly, "I haven't been much fun to be around lately."

"Hey," he kissed her forehead, "I understand. I just want you to take a break. I hate to see you so tired."

"Is that your way of telling me that I look ugly?"

Kael rolled his eyes. "No. It's my way of telling you that you need to have some time to yourself. Do something that relaxes you."

Gwyn knew what he meant. She was very sad, and he shouldn't have to see her that way. It was wearing him down too. She gently wrapped her arms around him, her eyes closing as tears threatened to spill from them. "This relaxes me."

Knowing that the weight of the world was on her shoulders, he wrapped his arms around her securely. It was too much for his Gwyn. Sure, she had the military and the president on her side. If it wasn't for their belief in her, Gwyn – and the rest of the country – would be entirely unprotected. But she was carrying the weight all by herself.

"I love you, Gwyn. You don't have to shut yourself down. I don't want you to build walls because you don't want me to know you're sad. I'm going through this *with* you. I want you to lean on me, alright?"

Gwyn nodded. The hug was helping. She thought that she might even fall asleep. But she heard something behind her. Hesitantly, she stepped away from Kael and saw Ana. "What do you want?"

Ana ignored her. She looked straight at Kael, pretending as if Gwyn didn't exist. "You must realize that we're preparing for a war as well."

Kael stood in front of Gwyn unsure of whether or not she needed to be protected. He certainly wasn't going to take a chance. "Yes. I know."

"Well, you're going to have to pick a side," she stood so

close to them that their noses were almost touching, her eyes ominous, "If you choose to fight with the humans. . . I'll kill you myself."

Gwyn let out a slow breath. She had forgotten that Kael's life was at stake as well. He was the one she was most concerned about. "Kael. . ."

"Wait," he said, his hand in front of Ana to separate her from Gwyn as he turned, "Do you still want peace?"

Was it going to be that easy? They had started this, after all. Gwyn had never wanted anything to do with their stupid kind. "Yes. . . of course. More than anything."

"You-" Kael pointed to Ana, "Wait outside. We're going to see my parents."

Ana shook her head angrily and waited outside the room. She would be able to hear everything that was said anyway. He had probably just done it to make Gwyn feel better.

"Alright." His eyes were so serious that it frightened her. Why was this information so important? "All aliens have power. They have immense strength and hearing. Their skin is tough to break through. And, they all have one power that makes them unique. At the age of five, they already have knowledge of *everything*. They are allowed to choose their one special power, so there's no telling what it will be. I suggest that you don't wait to find out."

"Kael, I –"

He held up his finger not wanting to be interrupted.

"Members of the royal family have a healing power. They can bring back the dead but only if the deceased have been dead under twenty-four hours. Royals can fight as well as anyone else, but they never do. They like to sit in their ship and watch. They don't like to be involved in battles. They let their people die for them. Remember, all the weapons we've designed will penetrate their skin, so they *will* die. Fire, blasts of energy, electricity, the strongest metal in the world –"

"KAEL!" She couldn't take in all of this information at once. She would have to process it later. It was just. . . too much. "Why are you telling me this? Couldn't it wait?"

"No, it couldn't." She didn't understand what his parents were like. . . what they were *all* like. His sister was the only alien he'd ever known to act remotely like a human. "You needed to know. . . in case my parents decide to take me away from you. My sister will bring you back here, but I may be trapped there. . . with them. . . forever."

She blinked several times, and it was several times too many. They couldn't waste any time. He had to take them before Gwyn had the chance to refuse.

"Trust me, Gwyn. Just trust me." Kael put a blindfold over her eyes. She wasn't allowed to see anything until they were where they needed to be. He had to beg Ana to keep her mouth shut. Kael didn't want Gwyn to have to relive any memories. She had probably seen parts of his ship before. He wanted to make this as painless as he could for her.

Finally, Gwyn's blindfold was removed. She had to blink again to adjust to the light in the room. It was brighter than any room she had ever been in. Other than her, there were four people in the room. Two were older, and one younger. She assumed they were his parents and his sister. They were dressed in silver, and all appeared to be human.

"My mother, Leah," Kael gestured to the woman who looked to be in her late-fifties, "My father, Gavin," he nodded to the man who looked to be in his early-sixties, "And my sister. . . Liza."

They all nodded at her from across the table. Gavin's hair was very dark gray. Not approving of this meeting, he was scowling at her. His beady black eyes were so cold that she had to look away.

Leah's hair was quite black and free of gray. Her eyes were spectacularly blue, and her face was kind. If Kael had inherited his looks from anyone, it would be his mother.

Kael sat down beside her and gripped her hand tightly in an effort to calm her racing pulse. It didn't help. She wasn't sure if she should speak or wait for one of them to. Gavin answered that question for her.

"How could you do this to us, Kael?" he said.

Kael's body stiffened. None of them seemed to care that she was sitting in the room with them. It made her feel. . . suddenly calm. So she squeezed his hand gently.

"How could you tell humans how to kill us?" his father continued. "You've given away our secrets, our weaknesses."

"How dare I make you seem mortal," Kael said coolly. "That's what this is about, isn't it? You don't give a damn what happens to me. Well. . . I have news for you. I don't give a damn what happens to *you*."

"Bite your tongue, boy!" Gavin shouted.

"No, I will not. I'm devoted to Gwyn now; she is my only concern. There was a time when I was devoted to *you*. Do you remember?"

"Why do you make it seem as though we asked too much of you?" his mother asked quietly.

"You left me to rot!" Kael stood, his hand still gripping Gwyn's. "I did what you asked me to, and you sent me to hell! I was alone, and you didn't care! So why are you so interested in me now?"

"Because you're about to destroy our civilization!" Gavin got to his feet too. Gwyn wanted to step in front of them. She had a feeling that that wouldn't go over very well. She would probably die.

"How could you betray us, Kael?!" Leah cried from the table.

"Would you stop it?!" Liza rose from her chair and looked from her father to Kael. "We are here to negotiate peace! You promised that you would listen to them, father! Instead, you're just taking this opportunity to put your own mind at ease!"

Gavin looked livid. He spun around to face his daughter; his voice booming with ferocity. "Your brother is a traitor! And, if you're going to side with him, you can be an outcast along *with* him!"

"You leave her alone!" Kael pulled Gwyn from her seat and led her to the door. She didn't need to be subjected to this any longer. "You taught us that peace was the better option over war. The only reason you're so eager to fight the humans is because you're angry. You're angry that I feel more at home *there* than I *ever* did with you."

The room was quiet. Gwyn felt like a mouse. Was she even in the room? At least Kael knew that she was there. . . she could tell because he hadn't loosened his grip on her hand.

"This is a phase," Leah said dreamily, "When you're ready to come home, we will welcome you back with open arms."

Kael didn't even look at them as he left the room with Gwyn. He made her focus on his face so that she wouldn't have to think about whether or not she had been in this silver hallway before. "I'm so sorry. Are you alright?"

"Yeah. . ." Gwyn was in a dream-like state. It didn't seem as though it had actually happened. "They didn't kill you. . . that's an up-side, right?"

Liza came out of the room and met them with a frustrated sigh. "They're just horrible, aren't they? So narrow-minded. . ."

"I don't know how you can stand it," Kael shook his head,

"I don't know how *I* could."

"Well. . ." Liza shrugged her shoulders and fiddled with her fingers. She was so confident yet. . . so nervous. "I just wanted to say that I'm so happy for you both. Your love is strong. . . I guess you already know that. Don't allow anything to separate you."

Gwyn wanted to go to sleep. His sister was so intense and surprisingly kind. How did she manage to be so much like a human with the parents she had? Either way. . . the impact of it all was draining. Perhaps it was something on the ship. "Um. . . thank you."

Liza gave Kael a quick hug before smiling as she watched them disappear.

Gwyn was very dizzy, and Kael had to catch her before she fell. He sat her down in her kitchen chair and made sure she drank a large glass of water and ate something wholesome before he was satisfied. "I'm sorry, Gwyn. I know it's exhausting. I'm an alien and *I'm* exhausted."

"That was pretty. . . surreal," she said slowly, "They looked so. . . so much like us. . . they even *behaved* like humans. . . we're so much alike, albeit we're enemies. . ."

"At least one person is rooting for us," Kael smiled sweetly. She couldn't help but smile back although the visit to the ship hadn't helped her mood any. As he stroked her hair and she stared at him sleepily, she hoped her dreams would be peaceful.

***

Gwyn was adding new paintings to the gallery. Much to her delight, they weren't dark and difficult to translate. They were bright and beautiful, just as they used to be. Kael was proud of her. He was glad that she hadn't given up on her artistic side because of the upcoming battle. It was also nice to see a side of her work that he hadn't before. It meant that she was happy. . . or as happy as she *could* be.

Katherine used any excuse to throw a party, and the gallery was the perfect place for one. Gwyn noticed that there were a lot of men present. Women were sprinkled here and there, but men were. . . everywhere. She couldn't help but think that her mother had done it on purpose. It would have been funny if it wasn't irritating.

"Oh! Have you met my daughter Gwyn?"

Gwyn tried to hide behind Kael as she heard her mother coming. It was too late.

Katherine approached them with a young man at her side. "This is Gwyn. Gwyn, this is Grant. He's a lawyer. Isn't he handsome?"

Gwyn tried to smile in a friendly manner. "Yes, he is. Unfortunately, I'm engaged. Sorry, Grant."

The look of shock on her mother's face was worth it. Kael looked just as flabbergasted. To say that they were engaged to be married. . . however untrue the statement was, it sent thrilled butterflies all over his body. He liked the sound of it. Engaged to Gwyn. . .

Katherine showed Grant around the gallery and Gwyn clung to Kael's arm. She didn't feel safe with so much testosterone around. "Sorry about that. I just wanted her to leave us alone."

His smile was very small. "I enjoyed it, actually."

Gwyn giggled cheerfully and kissed his cheek. "Would you love to be engaged to me?"

"I *would* love to. I'd be tickled. I'd be *honored*."

"Well, then. . . I guess I'll have to wait for your proposal."

There was nothing like a bit of pressure. He had asked for it. Did that mean that she wanted him to propose this very second? He didn't have a ring. . . it wasn't very romantic. Did she care? Did she want him to recite a poem and get down on one knee?

He was in wonderment the whole evening. He had to seriously think about what she had said. Once they were back at her place, he didn't feel so anxious. Gwyn was exhausted. He knew she wouldn't want him to propose when she was so tired.

"God. . . that was what this party was about," she said as she slipped off her heels, "She wanted to introduce me to all the available men in the city. . . when she knows perfectly well that I am *not* available. The nerve of her. . . "

"I don't know," Kael said as he stood beside her in the kitchen, "You might be happier with a normal guy. . . with a *human*."

She kicked her painful shoes away and sighed softly as she looked him straight in the eyes. "I wouldn't be, Kael. I know you've probably been thinking about this for a while, and I have too. And. . . I've come to the conclusion that you're the only one for me. I don't care who you are, what you are, or what you've done. I love *you*. You're the only one I want."

He wasn't satisfied by any means, but he wasn't going to carry on the conversation when she clearly thought that she had ended it. He chuckled quietly and kissed her gently as his hand ran through her smooth hair. "The feeling is mutual."

Since she was tired and thought that he must be too, she insisted they both change into comfortable clothing and sit on the couch. It was a nice night to sit and relax even if he was stuck watching chick flicks.

But she couldn't stop thinking and neither could he. Finally, she couldn't stay quiet anymore. "Kael. . . are you *really* happy with me?"

He frowned at her, having no idea what she was getting at. "Is something wrong. . . ?"

She shook her head. "I just mean. . . would you be happier on your planet? It seems like you're trying to get rid of me."

Kael blinked quickly. He hadn't noticed any change in his behavior. Had he been mean to her? Had he said something to make her believe that he wanted to go home? "Gwyn. . . I'm not trying to get rid of you. I'm looking out for you. I want you to be happy, and I want to make sure that you *are* happy with me. I want what's best for you."

"Will you stop?" she said desperately, "You *do* make me happy. I wouldn't be with you if you didn't, okay? Stop thinking like that. You are the only person I want to be with. Enough with these insecurities. If you want to leave me, if *you* would be happier without me, then go. I'm not leaving you, okay? I know that your family abandoned you, but I'm not going to. I'm here to stay."

Again, he wasn't convinced. The odds were against them. There were so many things that could go wrong. "Alright. I'm sorry. I still have to get used to all of this feeling, you know? It's strange to me. It's all new."

"I know," she said softly, "And I'm sorry if I snapped at you. But I'm not going to give up on you. I love you, and you love me. That doesn't happen every day. Not everyone gets to be so lucky. So let's stop being down about everything all the time and enjoy it. Sound good to you?"

Kael nodded, pulling her onto his lap. "Sounds like a plan."

***

Gwyn yawned as she heard someone pounding on her door. Kael was sitting up beside her, his eyebrows were raised and his hair a mess. "What the hell is that?"

"I don't know. I'm going to go hit them with a frying

pan." After throwing on a robe, she trotted down the stairs and opened her front door.

Standing in front of her was someone she hadn't expected to see-her cousin Allison. Her brown hair was covered in blonde highlights, and her hazel eyes were narrowed beneath her black sunglasses. She was chewing a piece of gum which sounded like bombs going off at this early hour. "Are you going to invite me in?"

Gwyn groaned and rubbed her tired eyes as she stepped aside. "Come in. . ."

Allison wasted no time bringing in the two suitcases behind her and setting them near the living room. Gwyn closed the door and followed her cousin into the kitchen, deciding that she should get started on breakfast. She wouldn't be able to sleep now. "Are you. . . planning on staying long. . . ?"

Kael walked into the kitchen clinging to his robe once he saw that they had company. His hair was still a wavy mess of knots. "Who is this?"

"This is my cousin, Allison . Don't ask me what she's doing here because I don't know." Gwyn made a pan full of eggs and buttered some toast, waiting for Allison to explain herself when they sat at the table.

Kael stuck himself to Gwyn's side sitting cautiously next to her as he watched Allison.

Allison gobbled down her eggs before saying a word. "You want to know why I'm here?"

He nodded slowly and tried to comb the knots out of his hair with his fingers. "That'd be nice. . ."

"Do you promise to make yourself presentable if I tell you?" she asked.

Kael blinked, and Gwyn frowned. "We weren't expecting company. We can have bed-head if we want to."

"Well, it suits *you*," Allison said snottily, "It just looks ridiculous on him."

"I like it. I think he looks cute." To further irritate her cousin, she ran her fingers through the opposite way that she had combed it making it almost stand straight up. "There. Now, tell us what you're doing here. You interrupted our beauty sleep."

Kael tried to fix his hair with Allison's eyes burning holes into his face. "Your mother sent me. She wants me to keep an eye on Kael. She doesn't think you're safe with him."

"I only kill people in the mornings. . . after they've woken me from my bountiful rest and made fun of my bed-head." When Allison dropped her fork, Kael smiled satisfactorily.

Gwyn giggled before kissing his grinning lips. "God, I love you."

"I love you more. . ."

"Don't start that!"

"Ugh," Allison rolled her eyes, "I'm going to throw up."

"The bathroom's *that* way," Kael jerked his thumb in the direction of the hallway.

Gwyn tried not to giggle again as Allison got up from the table. She was a *very* unwelcome visitor. "My mother--she's unbelievable."

"I just put myself in her shoes," he shrugged his shoulders, "If I had a daughter, I wouldn't want her to be dating an alien either."

Groaning in annoyance, she put her arms around his neck. "Do you mind if I move in to your place for a while?"

"Will I be able to join you?" he raised his eyebrows, "I won't be able to survive your cousin alone."

"Even if you *didn't* want to join me, I would make you come with me." She took his plate and hers once they were finished eating and set them in the sink.

They both jumped when Allison shrieked from down the hall. Once they realized what she had seen, they both smirked.

"EEK!" Allison washed her hands thoroughly in the sink; just *thinking* about what they had done in the bathroom made her feel dirty. "Why are there condoms in this trash can?! Do you have sex in the shower?! Why can't you use the bathroom UPSTAIRS?!"

"Because!" Gwyn shouted back at her. "We're not ashamed of our love!"

Kael laughed, getting up from his chair. "On second thought. . . maybe we could scare her into leaving."

***

No matter what they did, Allison wouldn't leave. Gwyn didn't really mind. She had just finished packing some of her things to move in to Kael's house temporarily. Allison was watching them with wide eyes as they took the boxes to Kael's car.

"You can't go! You'll get me in trouble with your mom!"

"You're a grown woman," Gwyn said, handing another box to Kael, "If you're afraid of my mother. . . you have serious issues. Don't you have someone else you should be taking care of? A little one, if I remember correctly."

"He's fine," Allison sighed, "Your mother has him."

"Oh, yeah. *That's* a healthy environment. Did she tell you that my father attacked us both?"

"Yeah, she mentioned that. . ." Allison said quietly. "Do you think that. . . the four of us could move in together? It's just. . . I think I'll get lonely without adults around to keep me sane, you know?"

Gwyn looked over at Kael. His eyes were wider than what seemed humanly possible. . . then she reminded herself. "Well. . . can we just have Kael meet him first? He's not used to being around kids. Frankly, neither am I. If we all get along, we'll live together for a while. Alright?"

Kael wasn't sure about the idea, but if he wanted to spend time with Gwyn, he supposed he could deal with a child running around. Besides. . . it would be a good time to figure out whether or not he was suited for fatherhood.

Gwyn had moved into Kael's house. The quietness was nice though Allison had been calling every day since they had left her. She was lonely and Gwyn understood that, so she had agreed to go to her cousin's house for a swim.

"Thank you for coming over, Gwyn," Allison said, waiting by the end of the pool, "I really appreciate it."

"Kael and I are happy to help." The two of them were waiting on him. They were in bikinis, and he was taking so long that it made them wonder if *he* was going to wear one too. "What the hell is he doing in there. . . ?"

Just as she said it, Kael came out of the house squinting his eyes as they adjusted to the light of the sun. He was in swimming trunks, and a towel was draped over his shoulders covering all of his chest. "You guys go ahead. I'll just. . . sit up here for a moment."

"Kael, you are getting in this pool with us," Gwyn said sternly.

"I don't want to. . ." He shifted the towel as if it would magically lengthen to cover the rest of his body.

"What's the matter with you? You're not. . . self-conscious are you?"

"Well, yes," he said awkwardly, "I can't remember the last

time I was this naked in public."

Gwyn rolled her eyes at him as she moved toward the towel to snatch it off. "I've seen it before. Allison isn't going to make fun. I highly doubt she's been with a man better looking than you."

"Hey!" Allison folded her arms defensively, "I've been with handsome men!"

"But have you been with men who look like this?" Gwyn pulled the towel off of her boyfriend, proud to see his beautifully toned body.

Kael tried to cover up his chest with his arms as Allison sighed enviously. "No. . . no I haven't. You suck, Gwyn."

To stop their gaping, he hopped into the pool, stood in the shallow end, and crouched so that they couldn't see his chest. "Go. . . talk amongst yourselves. Leave me alone."

Gwyn and Allison looked at the open door leading to the inside, hearing voices. Katherine and Joseph stepped out onto the pool deck with a little boy that Kael didn't know. He assumed it was Allison's son.

"Ali," Katherine said quietly, "We're sorry. . . we didn't know you would be here with. . . with them."

Kael hadn't given her any reason to believe that he was dangerous, so she scooped up her son with a smile on her face. "You remember Auntie Gwyn, don't you? She brought a friend for you to play with."

"Thank you, Auntie Gwyn!" the boy said excitedly.

"Um. . ." Gwyn looked over at Kael nervously, watching as the little boy walked over to him. "You're welcome, Johnny. . ."

They were all holding their breath. Joseph was ready to attack again. He was watching the two like a guard dog. Johnny couldn't have been more than five years old. His light brown hair was brushed neatly over to one side, his bright green eyes full of life. Kael didn't know how to react until the little boy was right next to him.

"Hi there!" Johnny looked down at Kael in the pool and smiled widely.

"Hello. . . Johnny, is it?"

He nodded. "Do *you* have a name?"

"Sure I do. It's Kael."

"Oh, your name is so cool! Can I call you Cool Kael?"

"I don't see why not. . ."

Johnny held out his hand, leaving Kael completely confused.

"Um. . . what's that for?" Kael asked.

"Well, I would give you a high-five, but I don't think you could reach because. . . you're down there and I'm up here."

"We can fix that." Kael helped Johnny into the shallow end of the pool and decided to stand up straight. Now he envied the little boy. *He* was short enough that his body was covered. Now Kael was exposed.

"Thanks, Cool Kael!"

"No problem. Since everyone else seems to be too scared to come into the pool. . . would you like to swim with me?"

Johnny chewed the inside of his lip and ran his fingers through the water. "I. . . can't swim."

He looked so disappointed. It was terrible to see him so sad. He was only a little boy. "I can teach you, you know. It may be difficult at first, but. . . *everything* is difficult at first."

"I can't do it, Kael. I'm scared just like everyone else."

"That's not true. *I* think you can do it. Do I strike you as the sort of person who would be wrong about these things?"

Joseph moved to snatch Johnny from the water, but Allison held up her hand to stop him.

Johnny looked at his mother, then back at Kael. "No. . ."

"You'll have to trust me then, won't you? You have to show the water that you're not afraid. Once you find a way to work with it, swimming's the easy part." How strange it was. He was explaining swimming to a child, and it sounded so much like his own situation. . . without the water.

"Okay. . . I believe you."

Allison sat with Gwyn and watched as Kael taught Johnny how to swim. They were getting along so well. Joseph and Katherine remained standing, ready to scoop Johnny out if Kael decided to drown him. Johnny didn't have a father figure, so it was understandable that he should want to bond with the nearest man around. Gwyn was glad that Kael was so good with him.

"He's a natural, Gwyn," Allison remarked, "Most *humans* can't even do this with a child. . . it takes someone very special. I don't care if he's an alien. I like him."

Gwyn smirked softly, glancing over at her parents. "I'm glad you do. I don't think *they* ever will."

"Eh. . . who cares?"

Johnny was quite proud of himself. He had no idea that Kael was an alien. He looked pretty normal. He was a lot nicer than guys that his mother had brought home. "Kael? Are you going to marry my Auntie Gwyn?"

Gwyn heard this and he knew it. He cleared his throat, ignoring that she was there. "Perhaps. . . someday."

"Do you like kids?"

"I like *you*."

Johnny smiled smugly. "When you have kids, I'll teach them to be just like me. You *are* going to have kids with Auntie Gwyn, aren't you?"

"Perhaps. . . someday."

His curiosity had died with Kael's uninteresting answers, so he climbed out of the pool and gestured for the man to follow. "Will you play tag with me?"

"I don't know how. You'll have to teach me."

Happy to be teaching something to a grown-up, Johnny took Kael around the back yard. The rest of them simply watched. Two of them were enjoying the sight. The other two were on edge.

"Ali. . . " Joseph said slowly, "You can stay with us again. There's plenty of room at our house. I think Johnny likes it there."

Allison was unable to afford her house payment. She didn't have a husband or a boyfriend to help her out. She wouldn't mind so much if Johnny wasn't so attached to the house. "No, thank you. We'll be alright with Kael and Gwyn."

The rest of the day was spent watching Kael and Johnny play tag and hide-and-seek. Gwyn's parents had left long before the sun had set.

On the car ride home, Allison had told Gwyn and Kael all about her money troubles. His mind was at work wanting to help her out in any way he could. No one knew that he had money. Gwyn had never asked him what he had done for the last few years on his own. He had done well for himself. . . considering.

Once they reached Gwyn's house, Kael carried the little boy upstairs and tucked him into a bed that was in a spare room. Allison thanked him for spending the day with her son, then she went to bed herself.

Kael walked downstairs with a smile on his face. This was what life was all about. Helping others. . . loving them. . . caring for a child in need of a friend. . . making a mother feel that everything was alright. *He* had done that.

Gwyn met him by the front door with a blanket in her hands. "Let's go get a coffee. It's a beautiful night. I can't bear to end it yet."

Kael nodded happily and walked out of the house. They walked to a café to get themselves a hot cup of coffee and then went to a park. The blanket was spread out on the grass, and they laid beside each other, their hands entwined.

"Which way is your planet?" Gwyn asked, her eyes wandering over every star she could see.

"I'm not sure, actually. . . it's beyond the stars you can see. Growing up, I didn't think it was far from Earth. Now that I'm here. . . it *is* a long way."

She was quiet for a while. Her thoughts kept urging her to ask more, but she couldn't bring herself to. What had his people done? Were there other species of aliens? There had to be. The question she most wanted to ask was. . . what had *he* done? Somehow, she knew it would tear them apart.

She didn't know if she could handle the thought of him torturing or killing someone- even another alien. It was. . . too awful to think about. Instead, she decided to ask a more innocent question. "Why did you fall in love with me, Kael? Out of all the other humans. . . out of all species of your kind. . . why *me*?"

Kael wanted to shoot himself for assuming that she already knew. Why did he do that? Why did he *always* assume? It must have been because he knew more about the world than she did. He knew about *other* worlds. It was about time he explained his feelings to her. "I could. . . sense your existence. I've been able to feel you since the day I was born."

Gwyn smiled tearfully at the stars. "Really?"

He nodded. "I knew that you were out there. . . somewhere. I just didn't know when you would come into my life. Instead of embracing it, I rebelled. I tried to escape it by doing terrible things. I guess I was. . . afraid to feel so much. No matter what I did, you were still there. And now that I've found you, I can't imagine being without you. I've done so many unthinkable things that I regret. . . but you make me feel like it's all okay. That it doesn't matter. That I can get past it."

She wiped a few of the tears on her cheek. She wanted him to go on. It was such an intense knowledge. How he was able to express himself. . . how much he truly loved her. . . it amazed her. "Please don't stop."

Kael gave her hand a gentle squeeze. "I can't think about tomorrow without thinking of you. When I look into your eyes, I see my life. I see my future. My atrocious deeds are washed away. Where I come from, I'm a prince."

She looked over at him. "You are? I think I'd forgotten that. . . "

"So had I. I didn't think it mattered. There, I have wealth and power. I could have anything I want. Here, I have you. And you are *all* I want."

Gwyn giggled softly and wiped her eyes before turning on her side to face him. He did the same, his hand lovingly swept across her cheeks to dry the remnants of her tears. "You are. . . spectacular."

Kael chuckled. "Thank you. You're not so bad yourself."

"I mean it. I don't think there's anyone else like you on this earth. . . I guess that's that point. I wish *I* could express myself so beautifully."

Maybe she couldn't say a thousand wonderful things to give his heart wings, but she had to try. "You have given me a reason to look forward to life. You are the one who inspired me to be strong-to move on and fight back. I thought that I was going to spend my life isolated and alone. You may think that I saved *your* life. . . but you really saved *mine*."

He kissed her tenderly; his hand ran through her hair. That was all he wanted to hear. That his love was returned. That this love was worth fighting for. . . that it was worth *dying* for. The world could look down on them. He didn't care and neither did she. Though – to protect the eyes of the innocent - they pulled the blanket on top of them.

***

A ball was being thrown for Gwyn's birthday. It was one of the perks of knowing. . . a *lot* of people. Kael was slightly nervous that he was going to be around so many people who wanted to kill his kind. Even the president was supposed to make an appearance. He only felt slightly better when he knew the focus wasn't going to be all on Gwyn. It was supposed to lift people's spirits too.

He was sitting at a round table with Allison and Johnny. Everyone was dressed nicely. The tables were covered in white cloths and the floor was all red carpets. It looked like the color of blood to him. . . but he wasn't going to say anything.

Gwyn was walking up to the stage to give a speech. Kael was playing tic-tac-toe on a napkin with Johnny. It was far more entertaining than anything else that was going on. Of course, when Gwyn cleared her throat as she held a microphone, he looked up at her. So did everyone else in the very large room.

"Good evening, everyone." She waited for the room to murmur an answer before she went on. "Because it's my birthday tonight, I'm told that I have to make a speech. I do have good news. . . and me turning a year older is not it." The room chuckled.

Speaking to so many strangers was unnerving though she had met most of them before, at least once. "There is no reason for us to fret about this war. Things have been quiet for a while and there has been no talk of battle on either side. The important thing is to remain calm. Devices *are* being made to prevent the aliens from entering our homes."

The room was excited. They were all talking, and then they clapped. She should have made more of a speech, but she took this as her cue to leave. "That's really all I had to say. If you would like more information, there are a number of military officers here that you can speak to. Thank you and have a good night."

Happy that the attention was off of her, she walked back to her seat and sat next to Kael. "Oh, God. I hate doing that. They expect me to sound intelligent and make long speeches. . . they have the president for that."

"You could be president!" Johnny said sweetly.

"Goodness, no," Gwyn smiled, "I'll leave that up to you."

"About these devices," Kael chimed in, "Are you going to have one of them?"

Gwyn scoffed. "What would I need one for? I have you to protect me."

"That's a relief. For a second there, I thought you might be glad to get rid of me." He stared at her lovingly for a moment then kissed her forehead before getting to his feet.

"Hey," Gwyn frowned, "Where are you going?"

"Not far. I want to give you your birthday present." Without waiting for her input, he walked onto the stage and a man handed him a guitar. Clearly, he had planned this ahead of time.

"Excuse me, everyone." When the room settled down, he sat down on a chair in the center of the stage bringing the microphone with him and setting the guitar on his lap. "I would like to dedicate this song to a very special woman. She knows who she is. I think we all do. This is for you, my darling."

Allison smirked at Gwyn and Johnny clapped excitedly.

Kael took a deep breath to calm himself, then played his very own melody on the guitar as he sang. "Screaming in silence. Perfect on the outside. The feelings are intense. Hiding beneath your pride. The stars may stare you down. The world may find you small. But you stand out in crowds. And I won't let you. . . I won't let you fall."

Gwyn was blushing softly as people started to look at her. How did they know? Was it because he was watching her with such adoration? Well. . . her loving gaze gave them away too.

"Wanting for too much. Memories that you can't have. Nothing will be enough. So why should you be so sad?

The world may stare you down. The fools may find you small. But you stand out in crowds. And I won't let you. . . I won't let you fall."

Gwyn hadn't even known that he could sing. Yet here he was. . . singing to *her*. She didn't know which she liked better. . . the song – or the way he was looking at her.

"When I wake up, I look for a face. And my own is not the one I see. It doesn't take much to feel out of place. Where you are is where I want to be. The world may drag you down. Don't mind who finds you small. 'Cause you stand out in crowds. And I won't let you. . . I won't let you fall." The guitar continued for a little while before the song ended. He was glad when it did.

Ignoring the clapping and cheering, he gave the guitar back to the man that had handed it to him; he walked back to the love of his life. "I hope I didn't embarrass you."

"Well, you did, but. . ." Gwyn smiled brightly as she took his hand. "It was worth it."

Johnny was clapping wildly. He had to have seen how happy the couple was together. Either that or he was very in love with Kael. Allison hoped it was the former. "Do it again, Cool Kael! Pleeeaaaaase?!"

Kael chuckled. "I will, as soon as we get home, buddy. Will you excuse us for a minute?"

Allison nodded. "Yeah, yeah. Go make with the smooches."

He was almost to the door when a man stopped them. He was a little shorter than Kael with large eyes as wide as they could be. His eyes were black and it seemed like his brown hair had been falling off in clumps. He looked crazed, in fact. "It's not right. I have to show you. You can't. . ."

The man trailed off and Kael was relieved when he simply walked away. Ignoring the interruption, he held on to Gwyn's hand and led her just outside the building. The stars were shining brightly as if they were giving him their blessing. This moment was why he had been nervous all evening.

Gwyn tilted her head questioningly, her smile unwavering. "What is it?"

Before he lost his nerve, he took a small box out of his jacket pocket. Inside was a diamond ring surrounded by gorgeous blue stones. Gwyn blinked at it, her heart skipping a beat. . . but it was a good thing. "Gwyn Farrow, I want you to marry me. Be my wife. You're all I want. You're all I need. You're. . . my everything. And you already know that. If you feel the same way about me, I want to be yours. . . forever."

How could she say no to him? He was everything to *her* as well. She had thought that he was going to propose the other night when they laid beneath the stairs. She didn't need an hour long speech about how much she meant to him. She *did* already know. His proposal was in his song. "Of course I'll marry you!"

Kael slipped the ring on her finger as quickly as he could, then he threw his arms around her and held her tightly. No words would ever express how truly happy they were in that moment. As he placed a passionate kiss on her soft lips, he knew that it couldn't last. . . not forever. But he would take all the time he was given.

Hours later, when he was sleeping soundly next to Gwyn, something woke him. Someone was crying. It wasn't Gwyn. Thinking that it must be Allison, he went to check on her. But Allison was sleeping. He walked through the house to find the crying person, and the sound finally led him outside.

He crossed his arms over his chest to protect himself from the cold. Ana was crouching on the porch her head in her hands and her body wracking with sobs. "Ana? What are you doing here?"

She didn't answer him.

"Ana. . ." He couldn't help feeling sorry for her. He had only seen her cry once or twice before. "What is it? What's wrong?"

Ana got to her feet. She sighed softly and clutched an object that was in her hand, pushing her emotions back to a place where she hoped no one would see them ever again. "I love you, Kael. . . and I'm sorry that I have to do this. You'll thank me one day."

Not having time to ask what she was talking about, Ana hit him over the head. When he opened his eyes again, he was in a basement. Because Ana was standing in front of him, he guessed that she had taken him to her house. When he tried to stand, he found that he was tied tightly to a chair. "How long have I been out?"

"Just a day," she yawned softly, "I was getting bored waiting for you to wake up."

"I'm sorry that kidnapping me is such an inconvenience." He rolled his eyes as he pulled against his restraints. It was no use. He was going to be there until Ana was tired of him. "Where's Gwyn? Does she know where I am?"

"Of course not, you idiot," Ana grinned at this, "That would spoil my fun."

"Fun? No. Don't have fun." What had he done? His thoughts kept rushing to the worst scenario. Was Ana going to kill Gwyn? Was she going to take her to their ship? To their *planet*? "You can do anything you want to me. . . just don't hurt Gwyn. She's innocent in all this. She doesn't deserve whatever you have planned."

"You're right," she said dreamily, "Gwyn doesn't deserve it. . . but *you* do. I'm not going to harm her psychically, Kael. I'm going to do *so* much more damage."

Kael furrowed his brow in confusion.

"I'm going to show her who you really are, my pet."

What did she mean by that? Was she going to show Gwyn what their lives had been like? She probably wanted Gwyn to be afraid of him. "Ana, really. Is this necessary? I'll tell her myself if you just let me go."

"Oh, no you won't. See, I'm going to *show* her the monster you are."

"The monster I *was*."

"You still are. Somewhere inside. . . you know it's true. Even if it isn't, she will always wonder what you're capable of. . ." Ana giggled mischievously. To his horror, with a snap of Ana's fingers, her appearance changed. Ana had taken on *his* appearance. She was going to pretend to be *him*! "Sit tight, lover boy. I'll be back to check on you."

"Ana, no!"

With a grin, Ana left her basement and walked out of her house. She was glad to be causing some misery. Looking like a man didn't exactly make her skin glow. But she wasn't just *any* man. She was Kael. . . and Gwyn wouldn't know.

She was forced to wipe the smug look from her face as she entered Gwyn's house. She could hear a little boy playing somewhere. Most importantly, she could hear Gwyn fluttering about in the kitchen. It felt so good to walk into the kitchen, and happy butterflies shot through her body when Gwyn smiled bright at her.

"Kael!" Gwyn gave Ana a hug, believing that she was Kael. "I woke up yesterday and you were gone. Is everything okay?"

"Oh, yeah," Ana hid a grimace; not liking the deepness of

her voice, "Everything's great. I had a little business to attend to."

"Congratulations, guys," Allison said from the table. Ana didn't know who the woman was, but they clearly knew each other. "Johnny is so excited about the wedding. I think he's hoping to be the ring-bearer."

"I think Kael would like that," Gwyn said as she returned to prepping a meal, "You two are bonding quite well. It's so adorable."

Who the fuck was Johnny? "Yeah," Ana said awkwardly, "That would be. . . great."

Allison giggled. "Wow. What happened to your vocabulary?"

Ana wanted to punch her in the face. If that one little act wasn't sure to give Ana away, she would have. It was difficult to be Kael! Especially because he had shut her out of his life. "Sorry. I guess I'm just tired."

"I know the feeling. I'm going to take Johnny out for the day. Your parents want an update, Gwyn."

Gwyn rolled her eyes and Allison got out of the house to spend time with her son.

Ana waited for Gwyn to finish her breakfast. It took a little while, but it was enough time to decide what she wanted to do.

"So," Gwyn said, "Can we start looking for wedding rings?

I want matching ones. . . except. . . yours can be manly. I wanted to look at dresses too, if that's okay?"

Ana rolled her eyes. "Can't you be happy with an engagement ring? I *just* asked you to marry me and you already want the world."

"Oh." She blinked. The Kael she knew would be ready and willing to give her the world if she asked for it. "I don't mean to rush you. I'm just. . . really excited. Girls always dream about their weddings, right? I'm ready for mine. I want to get married as soon as possible."

What the hell was wrong with her? Shouldn't she be picking up the nasty vibes Ana was sending out? God, she was selfish. "Would you stop thinking about yourself? Maybe I don't *want* to marry you so soon. Maybe I'd like to take a breather before we jump into spending the rest of our lives together."

Something was wrong. If he didn't look like her future husband, she would have sworn that it wasn't him. Still, what he said hurt her. It was unlike him to vanish for a day without a word. Usually, he couldn't stand to be away from her for that long. "I'm. . . sorry. . ."

She had better tone it down. She was being far too much like herself. She needed to convince Gwyn that she really *was* Kael for a little while longer. Long enough to get Gwyn where Ana wanted her. "I'm sorry, sweetheart. I'm very confused. It's like I woke up today a different person."

"Yeah. . . that's pretty obvious."

Shit. She was going to lose Gwyn. "I want to show you my world, Gwyn. Will you let me?"

Gwyn had been waiting for him to do this for a long time. He had always been so careful not to, but she wanted to know. What he'd done in the past didn't matter to her. "Yes, of course."

"Alright. Um. . ." Ana was so excited that she had to hide her grin with her hand. "Wait for me downstairs."

Why Kael wanted her to go in the basement, she didn't know. Perhaps he would be more comfortable there. Nodding quickly, she went into the basement and waited for him. She didn't know whether to be afraid or relieved that she would finally know about him.

When Ana came into the basement, she brought a young woman with her. Gwyn's eyes were so innocently wide that it was almost adorable. She threw the woman into a corner of the room then turned to Gwyn. She didn't want to waste any time, so she snapped her fingers, and Gwyn was tied down with invisible rope to a chair. "You're in for a treat."

Gwyn's heart was pounding. He *had* become a different person. "Wh-what are you doing?"

"You'll see." Ana grabbed the terrified young woman by the neck and put her at Gwyn's feet. She pointed one of her fingers and a blast of blue energy hit the woman. The poor girl screamed in agony as Gwyn watched in terror.

"This is what we do, Gwyn! We torture. . . we kill." Oh, she loved how that sounded with Kael's voice.

She couldn't believe this was happening. Why was he doing this? Had he been this way all along and she had been too blind to see it? "Kael, stop it! *Please!*"

Ana rolled her eyes and flexed her fingers, the blue energy disappearing. The girl on the floor was shuddering from the pain. It had left her weak. "You wanted to see the real me. Well, here I am."

Gwyn shook her head, *refusing* to believe it. It couldn't be him. . . this wasn't real. "Think about what you're doing! I don't know what's happened to you. I don't know why you're acting this way, but you have to stop. Please, Kael… for me."

Ana scoffed. "I'm done with you. You make me feel sick to my stomach. I can't believe I've been able to tolerate you this long."

"So you're going to punish this innocent person because you're mad at *me*?"

"Mm. . . yes. That's exactly what I'm going to do." Ana pointed her finger again at the woman on the floor, the blue energy shooting into her again.

***

Kael growled furiously as he struggled against his invisible ropes. Ana was extremely powerful. He had the same power of course; he just wasn't going to use it to hurt people anymore. He had to find Gwyn. He had to stop Ana before something terrible was done to Gwyn.

Ana trotted down the basement stairs and smiled as she shook her head. "You know you won't get to her until I let you."

"What are you doing to her?" he snarled.

"Oh. . . I just tortured a young woman until she passed out. You should have seen the look on your fiancé's face. . . she was so confused. . . so very terrified." Ana giggled.

For the moment, he was going to contain his anger. He wouldn't let her have the satisfaction yet. "You always loved to torture the innocent."

"I still do! I have to say, I'm not liking this look though. You're gorgeous, babe. But you're not me."

"So change back."

"Not before I've had my fun!"

Kael clenched his fists. "Ana, I am *begging* you. Leave Gwyn alone. It's me you want."

Ana's expression changed. He was able to see a glimpse of sadness. "Yes, you're right. I *do* want you. But I can't have you. And it kills me." Tired from the day's events, she spun on her heel and headed to bed.

***

"I-I don't want to die. . ." the tired girl whispered.

"You won't," Gwyn said uncertainly, "I'm sure he'll let you go soon."

"Do you know him?"

For the first time, she was ashamed to say that she did. "Yes. . . he's my future husband."

The girl blinked up at her from the floor. "How could you let him do this to me?"

"I. . ." What could she say to that? It wasn't her fault. . . was it? "I'm sorry. . . I didn't know. . ."

They both jumped when they heard someone coming down the stairs. Ana was getting bored with her victim. It had only been a day. She was usually amused for a few days at least. She was just rusty. "Okay, girls. Time for a little more fun."

"NO!" The girl clung to Gwyn's leg not having the strength to get up.

It made Ana grin. "I would tell you that I'm sorry, but. . . I'm not." Honestly, the pathetic girl should be grateful that she was going to be alive for one more day at least.

Gwyn was paralyzed. All she could do was watch the man she loved torture this poor woman. There were hours of screaming. The blue light made the girl's body convulse and smoke. She must have been in so much pain.

Gwyn's hands clutched the arms of her chair wanting to close her eyes but forcing herself to keep them open. She had to see what Kael wanted her to see. She had to know who he really was.

When the girl fell unconscious, Ana stopped her torture. She wasn't finished though. She had one more person to visit. "I'll see you two tomorrow."

Tomorrow. . . so there was still a chance that this girl would live. Maybe not a *good* chance but still. . . a chance.

Ana hurried to her own basement and grinned with satisfaction. She knew for a fact that she looked prettier than Kael did. He was black and blue from previous beatings. "God, that was great. Your poor little fee-fee was slouching in her chair wanting to be anywhere but in the room with me while I tortured the hell out of a poor girl. You know, I'm sure she was thinking back on your time together and regretting it."

Kael's heart sank. His poor Gwyn. She had dealt with so much. He couldn't blame her for believing that Ana was him. He had always made her wonder what he had done. It hurt him to think that she would ever regret being with him. "Why are you doing this?"

Ana sighed exasperatedly. "You know why. You're all I ever wanted. I am so in love with you, and you don't even see me."

"Yes I do, Ana."

"No you don't! Not like you see *her!*" He was getting her

worked up again. He was so good at that.

Kael closed his eyes and took a deep breath before opening them again. "I'm sorry, I never meant to hurt you. You know that I've changed. . ."

"That's why I'm so hurt. You wanted to forget about me, so you changed who you are!"

"It's not all about *you*, damn it!"

For a moment, she wanted to rape Gwyn just to spite him. But she was too disgusted to do that. She wouldn't lower herself to have sex with a human. "Fine. If you want to live like you're one of them. . . like you're a human. . . then you deserve to feel pain as they do."

Ana held up one of her hands. Red energy shot from it and into Kael's body. This power was only supposed to be used on humans. It would cause them unimaginable pain before they died - that happened within minutes. But because Kael was not human, the pain would last longer.

Kael gripped the arms of the chair as the energy surrounded his body. He couldn't move or even express the pain. That was part of the torture. No one knew what was happening. They could only see that the person the energy surrounded was in pain. But it shot through him; it was crashing into his veins and crackling against his bones. He may not have been able to use his voice, but on the inside, he was screaming. He was screaming like hell.

***

Allison was pounding on Gwyn's door. She would have barged in, but it was locked. All the doors were locked and so were the windows. Ana - deciding that she had better get rid of them - flung the door open and narrowed her eyes. "I told you, she doesn't want to see you."

"That's what you told me yesterday," Allison said, "I'm not leaving until I see her."

Johnny waved up at who he thought was Kael. Ana ignored him. "She doesn't want you reporting to her parents. Just respect her privacy and leave us the hell alone." Allison opened her mouth to say something, but Ana closed the door and locked it again.

When they didn't knock again, she headed back down to the basement. She had hoped that the torture would last longer. She just couldn't stand anymore. The whimpering, the crying, the begging. . . she had never been more bored in her life.

The girl was barely alive as it was. She was curled up at Gwyn's feet. Gwyn's eyes were exhausted. She kept trying to keep them open to watch for Kael. She kept thinking that he would snap out of his violent spurt and let them both go. She would never want to see him again, but at least she would be alive.

Ana looked at Gwyn then at the girl on the floor. "Time to wake up and die!" The girl's eyes snapped open. Because this power couldn't come from her body, Ana had to put a small device on her finger. To the eye that didn't know any better, it was a beautiful gold ring. Of course, it had been made to fit on her slender fingers. Kael's fingers were larger, and the ring only went around the tip.

She clenched her fist and cackled as she watched the girl on the floor shriek. Her eyes were melting away. Blood was pouring onto her cheeks. The girl tried to wipe it away before it got into her mouth.

Gwyn's stomach felt like it was dying. She felt like *she* was dying. How could her Kael do such a thing? He was killing someone. . . right in front of her.

When the girl's eyes were completely gone, Ana relaxed her fist before clenching it again. Now the girl's tongue was disappearing and blood poured down her chin. Gwyn had to close her eyes. This, she couldn't see. She couldn't bear it.

"Keep watching, Gwyn!" Ana kept her fist in a ball, her ears starting to hurt from how loudly her victim was screaming. "Yell as loud as you like, girly. No one can hear you. Courtesy of awesome alien powers."

Just as Gwyn's eyes opened, the girl's veins seemed to burst all at once. The girl fell to the floor. . . dead.

At the same time that Gwyn's heart was racing; its beating had also slowed. She wanted it all to be a dream - a nasty nightmare. Kael would never do something like this. She suddenly dropped to the floor beside the body having been freed from her restraints. She was going to pick up the lifeless girl when her body vanished. She looked up at Kael, breathing heavily with the effort of staying conscious.

The look on her face was all the payment Ana would ever need. "I can't let anyone find out what I did, silly. You're not going to tell on me. . . are you, Gwyn?"

Now that her senses had returned to her, she ran all the way past Kael, out of the house and to Ana's house without looking back. She doubted that Kael would chase her. He might be waiting for her when she got there though. Not stopping to take a breath, she flung open the front door and ran all over the house. "Ana! Ana, where are you?! I need your help!"

She paused to listen for an answer. When there wasn't one, she continued to the basement. But instead of finding Ana, she found. . . Kael. She blinked rapidly, shaking her head to grasp the image before her. He was passed out in a chair and looking as if he had been beaten to death. "What the hell is going on?"

Kael stirred in his chair, forcing his eyes to open. "Gwyn?"

She listened closely to his voice. This *was* Kael. The Kael that she knew. So, who was the Kael that had tied her up in her own basement? "You look awful." She quickly helped him out of the chair; her eyes scanned over him.

He took a deep breath as he leaned against her for support. "I'm surprised you could move me. She had me in invisible restraints; she must have dropped them."

"Yeah, me too." She had spoken too quickly. She didn't know what he was talking about. "Wait. . . *she? Who?*"

Her question was about to be answered. Ana trotted into her basement chuckling darkly while still in Kael's form. No longer needing the appearance, she snapped her fingers and changed back to her raucously beautiful *female* self. "That's better, isn't it?"

Gwyn wanted to faint. If she thought that Kael could catch her, she would have. "You did this?"

"That's right!" Ana flipped her hair; she was happy to be back to her own human form. "Kael didn't kill that pathetic girl. I did. I'm surprised you didn't know that I wasn't him. . . as far as I know, Kael's a new man! But he *has* killed before. . . in case you were wondering."

She *had* been wondering. She just wasn't going to say that out loud. "Oh. . . lovely."

"Will you leave us alone now?" Kael asked tiredly.

"Yes," Ana nodded, "I will. Because I know that this is the beginning of the end for you."

Ana stepped out of the way so that Gwyn could move passed her. Kael was still using her for support. She had to help him all the way back to her house. Then she set him in a chair and tended to what wounds she could.

"I'll be alright," he said quietly, "It'll take a couple of days to heal."

Gwyn gave a small nod. This had been so overwhelming. Her mind was still processing it. Shouldn't she have known that it wasn't Kael? Shouldn't she have known that the love of her life would never do something like that?

"You did know that it wasn't really me. . . didn't you?"

As soon as he asked the question, she felt like a knife had gone through her chest. She had to answer him honestly, but she was almost afraid to. "I don't know, Kael. I wish that I had known, but. . . I don't know what you were like before you met me."

He couldn't blame her, but he knew that he was making her uncomfortable. "Do you want me to leave?" He had to be a gentleman and offer though he didn't want to go.

"No," she said quickly, "That's not necessary. Besides, Ana might be tempted to grab you again. I don't want her to hurt you anymore."

"She hurt you too, Gwyn." He tried to touch her shoulder, but she pulled away from him.

It caused her physical pain to do that. It was an unsettling feeling to not have him touch her. She just couldn't. . . not right now.

Understanding where his place was tonight, he heaved a sigh and sat on the living room couch. That was where he would be sleeping.

A few days had passed and nothing was different. When he tried to touch her, she turned away from him. She was cold. . . distant. He had no one to talk to about how he felt. She had Allison over to sort out what was going on in her head. But Kael. . . he was all alone.

Gwyn kept her eyes on her coffee as she sat down at the table with Allison. It was awkward to be talking about Kael while he was just in the next room, but she had to talk to *someone*.

Allison had been filled in on what had happened. "So. . . how are you today?"

Gwyn shrugged. "We haven't really talked. . . or touched, since it happened."

"He won't even hug you?"

"No, no. I. . . won't let him touch *me*."

"Oh. . ." Allison nodded, her eyes moving around the room to avoid the subject as much as possible. But she couldn't. That was the reason she was there; to talk about it. "You're not okay. That's obvious. How's Kael doing?"

She felt guilty. She hadn't spoken to him, so she didn't really know how he was. She should have been getting her snuggles in as much as she could. . . but she couldn't bring herself to be any closer than a few feet away from him. "I think he's just as traumatized as I am. . ."

Kael stared blankly at the TV with Johnny beside him on the couch. He wasn't watching. He wasn't even thinking. He was. . . feeling. That wasn't something he wanted to do. It was difficult to avoid though.

Johnny didn't understand why they were all so quiet. No one would tell him what was going on. "So that wasn't you that answered the door?"

He shook his head. "Nope."

Johnny shifted nervously. "If it had been you. . . you would have been nice to me, right? You would have invited us in?"

How terrible this must be for such a small child. He understood that the little boy looked up to him. How could he explain? He was in a lot of pain. More pain than he could express to anyone - let alone a small boy. "Of course, Johnny. You know we would have had fun. . . if that had been me. I would have invited you in, and we would have played games. . . it would have been. . . a very different day. . . for all of us."

That made him feel better. "Could we play a game *now*, Cool Kael?"

Kael heaved a miserable sigh. "Not today, Johnny. Not today."

***

He couldn't take it anymore. She was crying every night - cozying up to a soft blanket instead of him. She wouldn't even look at him anymore. If he was causing her so much pain, he had to go. Without saying goodbye or leaving he a note, he dragged himself down the stairs and to the front door.

When he opened it, he saw the balding man whose insanity he had put out of his mind. . . the man who had stopped them right before he'd proposed to Gwyn. "I'm sorry, I. . . can I help you?"

"No," the man said through gritted teeth, "I have to help *her.*" He pulled a small gun out of his jacket; his hand slightly shook as he aimed it at Kael.

All he could do was blink. All he could think about was Gwyn. He would heal. Gwyn. . . would not. She was entirely human.

"Get in there." The man's hand was still shaking as he forced Kael back inside. "I have to protect her from you! She deserves better! I can't let you hurt her!"

He shook his head slowly. "If you're talking about Gwyn, I could never hurt her. I love her, man. She means the world to me."

"I felt the same way about my wife! I wonder if you remember her."

His wife? What. . . was this? It couldn't be. . . ? Oh. Oh, God, no. . . not now.

"My name is Albert Berry. My wife's name was Susan. . . and you killed her. I remember you. . ."

His heart sank as he held his hands in the air. "I remember you too."

Having heard the yelling, Gwyn rushed down to see what was going on. She stopped at the bottom of the stairs her heart racing in panic. "What is this? Who are you?"

"HE knows who I am!" Albert said, as he waved his gun, "He kidnapped me. . . and my wife. . . he killed her, and then he let me go!"

Gwyn narrowed her eyes in confusion. "When was this?"

"Ten years ago! I tried to tell people what happened. . . no one believed me!"

"I know," she said softly, "They didn't believe me at first, and now they know that it's true."

"And she's still not here with me!"

"Sir, please put down the gun."

That wasn't what Albert wanted to hear. "You're not defending him, are you?"

"I. . ." Gwyn took a step closer to him. "I can't let you hurt him. I love him, you see."

"Then you belong with him. . . DEAD!"

"No!" Just as Albert aimed the gun at Gwyn and pulled the trigger, Kael ran in front of her, and the bullet hit him in the chest.

Gwyn caught him as he fell to the floor while Albert, fearing that the neighbors would call the police, dashed out of the house.

"Kael?" she said quietly. "Are you alright?"

The pain wasn't as extreme as it would have been for Gwyn, but he was having difficulty breathing. He watched the door to make sure Albert wasn't coming back then nodded. "I'm alright. I'll heal. You'd better call the police before he has the chance to kill someone."

Gwyn let go of him and ran to the kitchen. Now that she knew he wouldn't die, she could call the police calmly. It didn't take the authorities long to find a crazed man who was waving a gun around.

She was dabbing away the blood on Kael's chest finding it hard to believe that this wound would heal. It had to hurt. The blood was very real and he should have been dead by now. Being an extraterrestrial really did have its perks.

She couldn't feel sorry for him now. Not after what that man had said. She found herself wishing that he would go home. She didn't want to be near him. At this moment, she didn't even *like* him. She knew it was time to ask him the question that had been stored up inside her since they had met.

"Is it true?" she asked quietly. "Did you kill that man's wife?"

He knew it was time too. Time to tell her the truth. Time to finally tell her what he had been so afraid to all this time. He could feel that she was pulling away from him. If he was going to lose her anyway, he might as well tell her. "Yes. I did."

That was what she had expected to hear. She had known for quite some time what her lover was capable of. She just chose to ignore it. "I want to know who you really are. I want to know what you've done. I want to know. . . what you've been hiding from me. No more secrets."

Explaining the life he had had on another planet was not something he wanted to do. But Gwyn wanted to know. He watched her closely as he spoke; he knew this would probably be the last time he would be allowed to see her. "Where I come from. . . royalty can revive anyone that has died as long as it's been under twenty-four hours. . . do you remember when I told you that?"

Gwyn nodded and urged him to go on.

"I started to revive the humans that we experimented on. If there were people doomed to spend the rest of their days on our ship, I sent them home. My parents didn't approve of course. They were going to banish me, you see, and I was afraid. . ."

Her heart was now sinking to the bottom of her chest. She nodded again.

Kael forced his eyes to remain on her face, his eyes full of shame. "I. . . I had to kill them. It was supposed to be my redemption."

She stepped away from him her eyes on the floor as she listened. Hadn't she known this all along? Couldn't she see it in his eyes? "No. . ."

"It was supposed to make everything better, but it didn't." He moved toward, her and she took another step back. His voice was becoming more desperate, pleading for her forgiveness though he knew he didn't deserve it. "I rebelled even more. I hated them for what they made me do. So I made them as angry as I possibly could, and they banished me anyway."

All feeling had left her. She was numb. What was she supposed to say to him? How was she supposed to handle it? "Did *they* suffer?"

"No," he said softly, "I gave your brother and sisters a quick and painless death."

He said it so smoothly-as if it was normal! As if that would make everything okay. . . "Get out of my house."

"Gwyn, please," he tried to take her hand, but she pulled away.

"Kael, I want you to go."

He could expect nothing less. He had murdered her family. He could have tried to help them even tell his parents to screw themselves, and let someone *else* do it. But, no. *He* had done it. "Can't we talk just a little while longer? I don't want to be without you. . . not yet. . ."

"I SAID GET OUT!"

He couldn't drag this out any longer, so he forced himself to move for the door. He didn't want to believe that he was never going to see her again. He needed something to hold on to. "Gwyn. . . do you still love me?"

The fact that he would even ask that disgusted her. Who did he think he was? He may be a prince on his planet, but he was the enemy here. "I did. . . yesterday. Before I knew that you killed my family." Gwyn opened the front door for him, watched emotionlessly as he walked out, and shut it when he was out of sight.

She had a bit of a mess to clean. Kael's blood had trickled onto the floor and onto one of her chairs. She had half a mind to leave it there as a reminder that he *could* bleed and that he *could* die. What a thing to think. This was the man - no, the *creature* - that she had agreed to marry. He had made love to her. He had proposed to her. He had killed her family, and now. . . she wanted to kill *him*.

How could she think that way? She never had before. Not too long ago, she couldn't even stomach the thought of Kael's death. She was filled with such rage. She wanted to tear apart her house, clean it up, and tear it apart again. That sounded like a brilliant idea at the present time. It would give her a little practice for the war that was to come.

Kael sat in the dark of his empty home. He couldn't even *call* it a home. There was nothing there for him. All of the happy memories he wanted to cling to were at Gwyn's house. He had no pictures of her here. No saved voicemail messages. Nothing that had her smell on it. Why hadn't he thought about those things before? He had taken it all for granted. . . and now it was over.

He could hear someone's footsteps behind him, but they weren't hers. He heaved a sigh, the familiar scent was both a disappointment *and* a comfort. "Here you are. Look upon me in satisfaction."

"You think I wanted this?" Ana said softly as she walked around the chair whilst looking down at him.

"Didn't you?"

"No, no, my pet. I never wanted to see you so unhappy. I think she broke you. How am I supposed to ride you if you're broken?"

"No one's going to be riding me anytime soon, Ana." He rose from his chair, his eyes tearing into her with all his anger. "Like you said. . . I'm broken."

"That's not such a bad thing, is it? You knew this day would come." As he walked away from her and up into his bedroom, she followed him. "Admit it, Kael. You don't belong here! I know that you wanted to fit in, but your reason for that is gone."

"Would you just shut up?" He slammed his door in her face, but he knew that wouldn't stop her. Sure enough, she popped up behind him.

"Come home, Kael. We all miss you. We all *want* you. You're not wanted here. . . you're not needed here. . . and you're not loved here. There's nothing for you and you know that."

Kael closed his eyes trying to hide his tears. He was ashamed of them. Talking to Ana again made him ashamed of his love for Gwyn. He was an entirely different man around Gwyn - a good one. Around Ana. . . he was who he *used* to be. That scared him. But it was all he had. It was all he could go back to. "Am I really wanted?"

"Of course you are! We all love you. You're our prince."

"One of many."

"None are so loved as you. It was why you were so distraught to be stranded here. Do you remember how you were when you were first banished?"

He nodded. It was quite fresh in his mind. "I nearly lost my mind."

"And who was there for you then?"

He sighed. "You were."

"And who is here for you now?"

Another sigh. "You are."

Ana forced him to look at her. She knew when to attack. Kael was vulnerable. He was weak. It was up to her to return him to what he once was. A monster. Now that Gwyn had kicked him to the curb, he would be all too willing to do as she pleased. "So. . . will you come home?"

He didn't really have to think about it. She was right. He knew she was. Gwyn was his only reason to stay. His only reason to *change* was Gwyn. If she didn't want him anymore, he had no other choice. "Yes."

She grinned evilly, her fingers tracing his cheekbones. "Don't worry, my love. I'll take your pain away."

Kael was so tired of having to process everything before

doing anything. He didn't want to think about how his actions would affect anyone. He didn't want to worry about what Gwyn would think. Forgetting his ex-fiancé, he allowed himself to kiss the lips of a woman he had come to despise.

***

He didn't want to admit that he was disgusted with himself, but he was. Ana had a way of getting into his mind and making him do what she wanted. He could still taste her mouth, still feel her body. It was meaningless. Uncaring, cold. . . and meaningless. He didn't want to be that person again. Ana was trying to infect him.

Deciding not to wait for Ana to wake up, he threw on some clothes and headed over to Gwyn's house. Even if she didn't want to see him, he had to try. He had to make her understand. He *was* the man she had fallen in love with. He *was* a man, no longer a part of his heartless race.

Once he was standing on her porch, he knocked on the door. He thought that she might ignore him, but it was a pleasant surprise when Johnny opened the door.

"Kael, you're here!"

He scooped Johnny up into his arms and gave him a big hug before setting him down. "Is Gwyn home, buddy?"

"Oh, yes," Johnny nodded, "They're talking about you in the kitchen."

He wasn't looking forward to walking in on them. Still,

Johnny let him in, and he hurried to the kitchen not bothering to announce himself before speaking. "I have to tell you something."

Allison looked cautiously over at Gwyn who gave her a small nod. She stepped out of the kitchen and sat in the living room with Johnny and strained to hear the conversation.

"Make it fast," Gwyn said heatedly, "I have things to do today."

Alright. It would be awkward to say so bluntly, but she clearly wasn't going to give him a lot of time. "I slept with Ana. Three times. You kicked me out three nights ago. . . and she hasn't left me alone since."

Gwyn blinked slowly; her eyes gave him a look that clearly said, 'you disgust me'. "That's a nice little detail. Do you want to tell me what positions you were in too?"

"You don't understand." Kael paced around the room knowing that he had to say the right words even if she didn't care. Just when he thought how to explain himself, she raised her voice just enough to let him know how angry she was.

"How could you do that? How could you sleep with her?"

He wanted to explain himself now, but the tone in her voice told him that Gwyn wouldn't really hear anything he had to say. "Well, it seemed to me like we were over. I had nothing left to lose, did I?"

"That's *twice* you've betrayed me," she said through gritted teeth.

"What else did you expect me to do?" he scoffed. "You said you didn't love me anymore."

"Well, you moved on pretty quickly." She threw her arms into the air. He had never seen her so mad. It was almost a relief. . . proof that she still loved him.

He stared at her; his eyes scanned over her every feature. He was looking at her for the last time again. . . would this time really be the last? "I was vulnerable. Ana manipulated me, it's what she does; it's what she's *good* at."

"Oh, that's no excuse." Gwyn turned away from him. She needed to calm herself. He wasn't allowed to see the pain in her eyes or hear it in her voice.

"I'm going home, Gwyn."

She slowly faced him again, the silence deafening. She knew what this meant. So did he.

"Unless you give me a reason to stay," he continued, "I'm going home. I know you don't want that. I don't want to do this, Gwyn. *Please.* . . please ask me to stay."

As much as she loved him, she had to stick to her gut. Kael was bad. She was against him. War was about to be declared, and she just couldn't see them fighting on the same side. "I can't."

"Stop being so stubborn." He walked up to her and looked

into her eyes, though she wouldn't look back into his. "You *can't* ask me to stay because of your beliefs. . . or you don't *want* me to?"

Gwyn refused to look at him. She didn't want him to see what she didn't want him to know. "Just. . . go."

He hated that she was being this way, but he had to go. As his fists clenched, he walked towards the door. To his slight surprise, a small voice stopped him.

"*I* want you to stay," Johnny said.

Kael sighed softly and knelt to the boy's level. "I wish I could. But I can't if Gwyn doesn't want me to. It wouldn't be right."

"But I'm going to miss you. . ."

The poor kid didn't understand. Kael was having trouble understanding it as well. "I'll miss you too, bud. I promise to visit though, okay? I'll be protecting you, even though I'll be away."

"If you promise, then I believe you." Johnny nodded solemnly.

"I'll see you later, pal." He gave Johnny a quick hug before walking out the door.

Allison was quiet for a moment. She knew that Gwyn didn't really mean to force Kael out of her life. "Are you sure that was the best thing to do? You were just angry. You still love him, and you might regret it later."

Gwyn shook her head. "It doesn't matter. We're enemies now."

Kael's head was swimming in thoughts as he walked to his bedroom. He couldn't bring himself to look at Ana. She would only make him feel worse.

"You didn't really think she would take you back, did you?" She had a smug smirk on her lips. She would tell him differently, but she so enjoyed seeing Kael in this kind of pain.

"Leave me alone." That was all he said to her. He knew that if he ignored her presence, she would leave. So he curled up into the darkest corner of his room. He wouldn't move from this spot until he was ready to.

**

Months had passed. He hadn't realized it. Sitting alone in the corner had made him lose track of time; everything blended together. He remembered Ana bringing him back to the ship. He had been given a room, so he'd found another corner to mope in. Ana came in to feed him and she was always irritated. Now he knew why. It had been happening for months. It was time for him to do something productive. So he got up from his corner and headed over to where he knew Allison lived. He wasn't going to see *her*. That would be idiotic. He had promised that he would visit Johnny though. That was what he was going to do.

He didn't want to look like a burglar, so he knocked on the

door. He was relieved when Johnny opened it. "Hey, you. Can I come in?"

Johnny titled his head in a confused manner, but allowed him to come inside. "My mommy's sleeping."

"Well, that's good. She won't make me leave then." There was an awkward silence, which he wasn't used to around Johnny. They were just staring at each other.

Finally, Johnny spoke. "Where have you been?"

Kael sighed. "I'm sorry, kiddo. I've been sad lately, and I didn't want you to see me like that. I also came to. . . warn you."

"Warn me? About what?"

"Now, I don't want to scare you, but something bad is coming."

Johnny was interested now. He sat on the floor and waited for Kael to sit next to him. "What's going to happen?"

"Well, I don't want to scare you, but you have to be prepared, okay? A war is coming."

Johnny blinked. "What if my mommy gets hurt? What about Gwyn? I don't want them to die, Kael. . ."

"Hey, no one is going to die." How could he comfort this kid? He couldn't guarantee that nothing was going to happen to the people he cared about. "Even though you won't see me, I'll be around. I'm going to protect all of you the best that I can."

Johnny nodded before throwing his arms around Kael. "I know you will."

As he appeared back in his room on the ship, he heard Ana's voice near the bedroom. Not being in the mood to hear what she had to say, he grudgingly walked over to her.

"Where have you been? You're supposed to be cutting off all ties with the humans." She sat up on the bed and glared at him as she turned down what their version of a television was - a glistening stone hung on the wall. Sadly enough, the quality was better than it was on earth. "The war is drawing near and you need to assure everyone that you're on *our* side."

He hadn't been listening to her. He was distracted by the sounds of the television. It was Gwyn's voice. His eyes were only focused on her, and he wished that it really *was* her. . . that she was there with him.

She was giving a speech. She looked very determined, very strong. It was nice to see that she wasn't losing her mind-not like he was. He touched where her face was on the glistening stone; his eyes scanned over every detail of her that he could see.

Ana rolled her eyes and popped up next to him disturbing his perfect silence as she whispered in his ear. "Are you ready?"

All he had to do was read her mind to know what was going to happen to him. His eyes still focused on the video of Gwyn, he shook his head. "Is *anyone* really ready to be tortured?"

Gwyn had just given a speech and was now having lunch with the president. They were sitting at a round table, and her parents were glad to help them fill it. They enjoyed every part of what Gwyn was doing and *she* hated every minute of it. It wasn't her. This wasn't what she was supposed to be doing with her life. She was supposed to be a painter. She was supposed to be getting married and having children. Kael had ruined all of that.

"We want you to negotiate everything since you know how to deal with these things," the president said, "I think we can agree that the first battle will be on U.S. soil. Soon, the whole world will be involved. But we may be able to wipe out a fair amount of them here. Then we'll know how they do things and we'll be ready for the next fight."

Things? *Things?* But they weren't just things. Not all of them anyway. Kael had been so kind and sweet. He had held her, loved her, *made* love to her. Some part of them had to be plagued by humanity. They had to think and feel just like humans did. . . didn't they?

"Gwyn," Joseph said roughly, "Are you listening? The goddamn president of the United States is talking to you and you're not even listening."

"Joseph, settle down," Katherine said quietly, "It's a lot to deal with. We know this is hard for you, Gwyn."

"Hard for her? She betrayed our country. She's lucky we're

even talking to her."

Gwyn was about done with her father. It was clear that he needed to cool off, so she poured her glass of water onto his head. He was astounded and angry, *very* angry, but he wasn't going to make a scene with the president next to them. "Can I talk now?" When he said nothing, she turned to the president. "I *was* listening. I understand everything. I will negotiate with them."

***

This was not how someone should be tortured. It was like he was in the middle of an arena. Now, it wasn't like everyone on his home planet was watching him live. It was only the people in his city. That was how they separated when they traveled. They moved by city. So it was just his city that was going to watch the event. Oh, this was going to be fun. They were going to enjoy his screams.

He looked over at his mother, father, and sister who had front row seats. His sister was the only one who cared. She couldn't look at him. That was fine. At least he knew that there was one person who wouldn't be watching him.

Ana had a smug smirk on her face as she strapped him into his chair. He rolled his eyes at her. He was supposed to be her one true, love and she was actually getting off on this.

"You look awfully happy about this," he said grumpily.

"Oh, you know I love a good torture. . . even if it *is* you I'm torturing." Once she was finished securing him in his chair, he stepped away to make her little announcement. "This is your prince!"

It was odd to him that they cheered at this, but he tried not to roll his eyes again as Ana continued.

"Though he is loyal to us now, he has betrayed us twice! Your king and queen have been generous enough to show him mercy. He will not be killed. But he must be made an example!"

They cheered again. If he could just. . . escape. If he could be anywhere but here. He didn't want to scream. He didn't want to cry like a baby when she tortured him. He wanted to be with Gwyn.

Ana tried to contain her excitement as she turned back to Kael. "Sorry about this. Torture is my specialty. . . and I can't say no to my duty."

Kael raised an eyebrow. "Will you be gentle with me?"

Ana laughed loudly. "Am I ever?"

Before Kael could answer or even given her a look of disapproval, he could feel the pain shooting through him. It felt like liquid fire in his blood. He was very proud of himself for not screaming- especially when the pain spread to his head, but he did close his eyes. He sank deeper into his body until he couldn't see anything. . . until he couldn't hear what was being done to him. Then he saw it. . . a garden of some sort.

His first thought was, *why the hell am I in a garden?* But it was better than feeling the pain. It was bright here. . . and warm. There was a tree growing bright red apples and a stream of sparkling water next to the tree. He didn't know where he was and he didn't care. It seemed to complete this place of peace when Gwyn appeared beneath the tree.

She blinked up at him not knowing how she had gotten there but sharing his attitude.

"They're hurting you," she said softly.

"It's alright," he said before sitting beside her, "I'll live."

***

Gwyn screamed as she sat up in bed. She looked over at her clock and it was about five in the morning. She had had a long day, so she was going to sleep in. Something had woken her. As the beads of sweat rolled down her forehead, she tried to remember her dream. It hadn't really been a dream. It was as if her spirit had left her body for a few hours. . . she was comforting someone. . . .she had been comforting Kael.

Then she heard Johnny screaming down the hall. He and Allison had been spending a lot of time at her house, so she just invited them to stay for a few days. She walked into his bedroom to find Allison already at her son's side.

"I – I had a bad dream," Johnny sobbed.

Allison looked up at Gwyn. She hadn't seen him this upset since he was a toddler. "What happened, sweetie?"

"It was Kael! They were hurting him!"

Alright, this wasn't just a coincidence. She and Johnny were connected to Kael. It was possible that he was trying to escape whatever was happening to him. It didn't make sense that he would make Johnny this upset on purpose though.

"It's okay," Allison said, giving him a tight hug.

"I'm worried," Johnny sniffled, "What if he's hurt?"

"I'm sure he's fine," Gwyn lied. They all knew that something was wrong. They were just trying to make themselves feel better.

Meanwhile, Kael was resting in a recovery room. He was covered in gashes and bruises. The least they could have done was give him a hot bath or something. It wouldn't have been the best thing for his gashes, but damn it, he wanted a hot bath.

He was so weak and in so much pain that he couldn't move. He could look around the room. . . .and that was it. He was glad when he noticed that Liza was sitting next to his bed. "Hello, Liza. That was some show, wasn't it?"

Liza shook her head. "I'm so sorry, Kael. I tried to talk them out of it, but they wouldn't listen to me."

"Hey, it's not your fault. Neither of us expected me to become the complete opposite of who I used to be."

"Are you. . . nervous about the battle?"

He would have shrugged if he could. "I've fought wars before. I think I can handle a battle."

"I don't understand it. Royalty isn't allowed to fight. We hide in our ships or stay home on our planets. We let others fight for our cities. . . so why do they let *you* fight?"

"Because. . . they've always known that I don't belong here. They were hoping that I would die in battle so that they could wash their hands of me."

"How can you do it, Kael? How will you be able to fight? I thought you liked earth now. . ."

"I do. Fighting would be a great way to let my emotions out. I don't want to hurt anyone though. I'll be alright. I'll get over it. . . somehow."

"Kael!" Ana smiled cheerfully as she stood by his bed and dismissed Liza with a wave of her hand.

Liza was so frustrated by Ana's presence that she left them alone without a fuss.

"I don't want you shooing people away from me. My sister is the only other person who visits me, and *she's* the nicer one."

Ana pouted her lips. "Do you *want* a nicer lover?"

"Is that what you are, Ana? Don't you have to be *capable* of love in order to be someone's lover?"

She scoffed at him. "I *do* love you, Kael! Just not in the

pathetic way that Gwyn does."

"It isn't pathetic. It's real love."

"Yeah, that's why she threw you out." She didn't want the argument to go any further. She really wanted to have a relationship with him again, so she made a mental note not to mention that bitch anymore. "When you're feeling better, we need to discuss new weapons." When he said nothing, she left his room.

***

Gwyn wouldn't admit it, but she was worried about Kael. She wanted to know if he was alright. She didn't know how she was going to find out. The only way she knew of would be going to his house. If she was lucky, he would be there.

When she stepped through his front door, she was sure that he had abandoned it. For one thing, it was trashed. Someone had gone through a lot of trouble to make it a mess. Another thing- not a single light was on. It was so dark that she could barely see what was in front of her. She was kicking herself for not bringing a flashlight.

She searched through nearly the whole house. There was no sign of him. She still needed to look in his bedroom. Part of her didn't want to; she was afraid that he might be in bed with Ana. She didn't want to see them in bed together. It would give her more nightmares.

There he was. He was sitting in a corner of the hallway by his room. She couldn't really see his features, but she knew it was him.

"I thought you were gone," she said.

"Sorry to disappoint," he answered without looking at her, "This is still my house."

"Right. So. . . who trashed it?"

"I did."

Gwyn rolled her eyes. "Of course you did. Why are you sitting on smashed objects?"

"I can sit wherever I want."

"True. I just want to know why you're on the floor when you could be on your bed."

"I can't bring myself to go in there."

Oh, so this was the part where she was supposed to feel sorry for him? He could cry her a river for all she cared. "Maybe you should have thought about that *before* you screwed Ana."

"I don't care about her, you know. She's just someone to pass the time with."

"Does Ana know that?"

"Does it look like I care?"

"Well, I can't *see* if you care because you won't look at

me!"

She wanted to see his face? That was fine. He got to his feet and took a step toward her; his battered face was in view. "Why are you here, Gwyn? Have you come to torture me? Is this fun for you?"

Gwyn blinked at him. Was he aware that it looked like the house had shown him a lesson after he'd trashed it? He looked horrible. His face was covered in cuts and bruises. She was sure that she would be able to see more damage if he was less clothed. "I was. . . looking for information. . ."

"Of course you were. It's always work with you, isn't it? You can't let yourself live for one second."

"Kael. . . what happened to you?" She had to know. She had to know why she'd had a dream about him. She had to know why *Johnny* had had a dream about him.

"Do you really care?" Kael scoffed.

"I wouldn't ask if I didn't, okay?"

"If you must know, my *people* did this to me. So while you're snooping around my house for information, keep that in mind. I have no reason to give away your secrets. I have *no* reason to be loyal to them."

She was getting angry. She hated to see him in such bad shape. Then again, he was the enemy. Why did she have to be torn with everything that had to do with him? "Then why did you go back home?!"

139

"Because I have nothing left! You left me with *nothing*! There is *nothing* for me here! You know that, damn it!"

"This song and dance is getting old, Kael! Why can't you just choose a side already?!"

"You're making it IMPOSSIBLE!"

"That's it." She turned around and walked back down the stairs and shouted loud enough for him to hear her. "I'm sick of you yelling at me. I wish you'd just make this easier on the both of us."

"Yeah? Well, *I* wish that YOU could make up your mind!"

As soon as she was out the door, he took whatever was still in one piece and broke it. He had left a few things precisely for this reason.

Ana found him breaking the remainder of his belongings and she giggled. "Now this is what *I* call a romantic getaway. Can I assume that Gwyn stopped by?"

"Assume away." He threw one of his framed paintings onto the floor and broke it with the end of a lamp. "Why can't she just leave me alone?! She wants me out of her life, but she keeps coming into *mine*! How am I supposed to forget about her when SHE WON'T LET ME?!"

"Oooh, I like it when you're angry." She giggled again and stopped him from tearing apart his couch. "They want to restore you as prince, my pet."

"Yeah. . . well. . ." He threw down his lamp and looked

regrettably at the unharmed couch. "At least *someone* wants me."

"*I* want you. . ."

He was still so angry. He wanted to do something self-destructive. . . and he knew that Ana wouldn't mind. He grabbed her by her hair and pulled her in for a rough kiss. She shoved him into the nearest wall careful not to irritate his more serious wounds as she tore off his shirt.

Gwyn slammed her front door and stormed into the kitchen as she tried to calm herself before she taught Johnny bad habits.

Allison looked up from her dinner plate at the table. "Hello. . ."

Johnny put his fork down. "Did you see Kael?"

"Yes," Gwyn said as she sat down, "I saw him."

Allison took over the conversation. "Okay. I take it that things didn't go well. . ."

"No, they didn't. We had another fight. His house looks like a tornado's been through, he's got cuts and bruises, and then he started yelling at me!"

"Are you. . . you know. . . actually over this time?"

"Duh," Gwyn scoffed, "We're finished. If we saw each other again, we'd just get into another fight. There's no point."

"Well, do you mind if we stay with you. . . indefinitely?"

Gwyn said. "Yeah, that's fine. I'll need the company anyway."

***

Kael looked around the dinner table and wanted to wrinkle his nose at the current company. God, they were a sight. His whole family was there. Cousins, aunts and uncles, some people he'd never met. . . only his immediate family was kind enough to wear their transmitters. They knew that he preferred to look like a human rather than an alien.

Ana was sitting beside him. He didn't mind because he knew it had to be done. She smiled at him. "Are you okay?"

He chuckled as he picked at his food with his fork. "I'm great. I was actually in the mood for a burger and fries tonight. . . instead, I get something that resembles squid and something else that's green and resembles noodles. . . with extra slime."

Ana giggled – a good sign. She didn't know what he was up to.

"Kael," one of his distant relatives cooed, "When are you and Ana going to get married?"

Kael didn't answer. He wasn't ready for marriage let alone marriage to *Ana*.

Ana knew that he wasn't ready for marriage just yet, and

that was perfectly alright. She took his hand and smiled politely at his relatives. "We're going to wait."

"What about children?" Leah asked, "I would like to be a grandmother before I get too old to pick them up."

Kael was glad that Ana's parents couldn't make it. They wouldn't have insisted that he marry their daughter; they would have *demanded* it. "Can I settle in to my life first?"

"My darling boy, you should be settling *down*."

He wanted to throw his food at everyone in the room. He wasn't sure how much more of this he would be able to take.

***

Gwyn was sitting with her parents and the president. . . again. These meetings were getting boring, but hey; she was supposed to be saving the world, right? It had to be done. She really needed to be paying attention; she just couldn't bring herself to. It was horrible, but Kael kept coming into her thoughts.

"I understand that we're asking a lot of you, but you were the reason we found out about these things in the first place," the president said, "We're counting on you to help us through it."

There was that word again. . . *things*. He was starting to get on her nerves.

"We want you to train our troops, to lead them," he

continued.

"You want *me* to train your troops?"

"Of course! You told us about their weapons, you told us all that you know about them. This battle will be small compared to the others, I think. You can handle this."

"No." The president stared at her as did her parents. They hadn't expected that answer.

"Excuse me?" Joseph asked.

"I'm sorry. I think I've done enough. I don't want to lead *anyone* into battle. I don't even want to be involved in the battle, but I don't really have a choice, do I? So, no. I'm not going to do any more than I have to."

"We're very sorry," Joseph turned to the president, "Our daughter needs time to think this over."

"Honey," Katherine chimed in, "I don't think she's going to change her mind. . ."

"Then we will change it FOR her."

Gwyn shook her head. They couldn't force her to do anything. They wouldn't understand her reasoning.

***

Joseph was dragging Katherine along on his errand. She was too frightened and worn to the bone to say anything, so she didn't complain. If she stood up for herself or her daughter, she would be punished for it.

Joseph knocked on Kael's door, praying that he wasn't there. He nodded gratefully when Ana opened the door. "Kael isn't here, is he?"

"No," Ana said hesitantly as she wondered what the hell they had come here for, "He isn't. And I don't very much like to speak to humans, so –"

"We haven't come here on behalf of Kael. . . we're here because of Gwyn. She's told us about you, and if you're anything like she says, I think you'll want to help us."

She was merely letting them in out of curiosity. If she didn't like what they had to say, she would kill them after their chat. She showed them inside and sat them down. "What is it?"

Katherine let Joseph do all the talking. She didn't agree with this. "We want Gwyn to think that Kael is dead. She has responsibilities and all she does is think about *him*. I think that if *you* tell her that he's dead, she'll believe you."

Oh, this was marvelous. She would be causing pain and Kael wouldn't know anything about it! She wasn't going to harm the bitch physically, but this would be much worse! She knew very well that Gwyn still loved Kael, and she wanted the worthless human out of her hair. If she happened to help this man in the process, so be it. "I'm sure Gwyn will come running back to Kael soon. . . but he's abandoned this house, you see. . . so she'll find me instead."

"And. . . that's when you'll tell her?"

"Yes. . . yes, I will."

***

"Allison!" Gwyn sounded hysterical. "I need your help!"

Allison came running into the kitchen. Except for her hurried pacing, Gwyn looked alright. "You almost gave me a damn heart attack. What's the matter?"

"I've been rethinking this whole thing with Kael. . . I mean, he's all I think about. . . and I pushed him away!"

Wanting to smack her cousin upside the head, Allison raised her eyebrows . "So. . . what? You want to go back to him?"

"Yes!" Gwyn stopped her pacing; her expression was desperate. "Is that terrible of me?"

"No, it isn't. If you love him and he loves you, you should be together. A lot of people never find true love. You did. You can't let it go."

"Why didn't you tell me this sooner?"

"Because you wouldn't have listened."

Gwyn hugged Allison tightly before running out to door and going to Kael's house. She felt. . . good. She felt energized. She was jittery and excited. She only hoped that he would forgive her.

When she went to knock on the door, she saw that it was open. She could hear voices inside, but one was a female, and the other was not Kael's. She stepped inside and glanced at the place. It was clean. . . and it was redecorated. Then she saw Ana and knew why. They were probably living together.

"Oh, right on time!" Ana giggled and walked over to Gwyn. She shooed the male in the room after asking him to move furniture.

"What's going on?" Gwyn asked. "Why are you moving his things?"

"Well, they're not his things anymore."

Gwyn looked surprised. "He sold the house?"

"No, no, silly. He died."

"N-no. . ." She stumbled backward into a chair and knocked it over by accident. What did she mean he *died*? He couldn't be dead. It hadn't been too long since she'd last seen him. He had been pretty banged up, but he didn't look like he was about to keel over. He was strong. . . he was determined. "H – how. . . how did it happen?"

"His parents got word that he had another visit with you. It just wasn't acceptable, so he was tortured again. . . he didn't survive his injuries."

Tears streamed down her cheeks though her voice was steady. "You don't seem too broken up about it."

"Hell no. Don't get me wrong, Kael was a blast. But there are other fish in the sea." That was a lie, but Gwyn wouldn't know that. Kael was all she wanted. He was all *she* thought about. She had to have him all to herself.

"There will never be anyone else for me. . ." Gwyn stood still for a moment, letting it sink in. She had been cruel to him. She had been unfair. Yes, he lied to her. Yes, he killed her brothers and sisters. But he had changed. . . she knew that. . . and she loved him, despite all his wrong-doings. She loved him and he was dead.

"Do you need proof, honey-pie? I can show you video from his funeral. . ."

"No, don't." She didn't want to see how hurt he was when he died. She didn't want to see what they had done to him. . . what *she* had done to him. Her last image of him; bruised and broken, bitter and hurt.

"Can you leave, then? I have work to do."

Gwyn ran home. She couldn't let Ana see her like this. She looked weak, and without Kael, she *felt* weak. She shut her front door and fell to her knees in the middle of her living room. Her breath hitched in her chest as she tried to breathe. *He died.* . . it kept repeating in her mind. Ana had said it so coldly. How could she be so cold when he was gone from the world? When she was able to breathe again, sobs shook her body as she buried her face in her hands.

Allison came into the living room with Johnny at her side. "Gwyn, what's wrong? What happened? He didn't hurt you, did he?"

Gwyn looked up at them. Her sobs stopped momentarily. She couldn't look at them for long. She began to sob again, her face going back into her hands.

Allison blinked at her. She wrapped her arms around Gwyn, hugging her as tightly as she could. Johnny knew what must have happened. Although he was angry at Gwyn because he wanted to see Kael, he hugged her all the same.

***

"We want to see her," Joseph demanded.

"I told you, she won't come out of her room," Allison sighed, "She's locked herself in there. She hasn't eaten since. . ."

Katherine looked at her husband immediately wanting to tell Gwyn that it was a lie and that she didn't need to grieve. But Joseph glared at her as they followed Allison up to their daughter's room.

"Gwyn," Allison knocked on Gwyn's bedroom door, "Will you come out? Your parents want to see you."

Gwyn didn't answer.

"Gwyn," Allison knocked again, "Please, sweetie. . . come out. You need to eat something."

"Move." Joseph shoved Katherine and Allison out of the

way then kicked in the door. "Gwyn, stop moping and get out here!"

Allison pushed him away from Gwyn's room. "You leave her alone. She doesn't need you to be an asshole; she needs you to be her father." She went to Gwyn - who was in a corner - and knelt beside her. "It's okay, you don't have to see them if you don't want to. . . but please eat something."

Gwyn still didn't answer. In fact, she didn't respond in any way. She wasn't moving. She wasn't even moving her eyes. Allison would have thought she was dead had she not been breathing.

"Gwyn. . . can you hear me?"

Still. . . nothing.

"What's wrong with her?" Katherine asked tearfully.

Allison shook her head. "She's catatonic."

***

Kael had just been re-crowned as prince. It wasn't complicated. All his parents had to do was announce that they forgave him and that they were accepting him back into the city. A crown made by human slaves was upon his head and all was right with the world. . . except it wasn't.

He didn't want this. He wasn't meant to sit on a throne and have other beings do everything for him. Being in the action wasn't difficult, but he couldn't do that anymore-not openly anyway. He had to save the world quietly. . . one human at a time. It killed him that he couldn't do more.

Ana was having a much better time at the celebration. She was eating and drinking enough for the two of them. She was all smiles even though Kael hadn't displayed a single emotion. "Say, Kael. . . when do you plan to make me your princess?"

Everyone's heads, tentacles, and whatever else they had, turned towards him. She loved putting him on the spot. He cleared his throat nervously. "I, uh. . . don't want to be pressured into marriage. I want to do it when it's right for me. . . for both of us."

They seemed satisfied with this answer because they went back to their food and conversations. Ana, however, was *not* satisfied. "We've known each other long enough. Never mind the years we were apart. Do you want to marry me or not?"

"Of course I do." It was a lie, but he had been working on those lately. He'd gotten so skilled at lying that even *he* believed it. "You know I do. I just don't think I'm ready right *now*. Can't we wait a while longer?"

Ana shook her head though she lowered her voice. "We can wait to announce it. . . but as of now, we're engaged."

She gestured for him to follow her out of the room. He didn't entirely want to, but he didn't have a choice. He had to keep up appearances. It was a very small sacrifice to make if he was thinking about the world and a very *large* sacrifice if he was thinking about Gwyn. It would all pay off in the end.

Now that he was officially their prince again, they would trust him and they wouldn't be watching his every move. It was quite stupid of them, really. Now he could do whatever he wanted.

Later that night, while he was lying beside Ana and thinking about Gwyn, he heard someone enter the room. He threw the sheet over Ana - who didn't like to be covered even when she was naked - and turned on a light. "What's going on?"

"It's Gwyn," Liza said, "I. . . I thought you should know."

He was thinking the worst. Was she dead? She had to be. Why else would Liza look so worried? "What about her?"

"She's catatonic."

Well, at least she wasn't dead. Too bad he couldn't show his relief. "Oh. . ." He looked over at Ana, who was now smirking at the two of them. "I'll assume this was *your* doing."

"Alright," Ana giggled, "I confess. It wasn't *all* my fault. Her parents helped. I told her that you were dead."

He sighed exasperatedly as if this was a chore. He couldn't show how furious he was either. "You really need to get a new hobby." After he got dressed and left Ana's room, his fists clenched immediately. "Do you think she's mad that

I'm going to help my ex-fiancé?"

Liza shrugged her shoulders. "I don't think so. She knows you'll always care about Gwyn." She looked around to make sure they were alone, then led him away from Ana's door and lowered her voice. "She's not onto you yet."

"And you are?"

She nodded. "I know. . . and I think it's very brave of you. You're a good person."

"We're not people, Liza," Kael sighed as he began to fade, "We're aliens." He appeared in Gwyn's bedroom; his heart raced.

He didn't know why he was so nervous. It wasn't like she could say anything to him. That was why he was here, wasn't it? And as soon as he helped her, he was going to leave again.

He walked up to the corner where Gwyn was seated and ignored her father's protests. Joseph, Katherine and Allison were all in the room. Their energy was all over the place and it wasn't going to help Gwyn any. Before he got too close to her, he could see a purple bruise that was on her cheek. "What the hell is this?"

Allison stepped away from Joseph and Katherine. "Joseph thought that it might make her snap out of it."

His blood was boiling and it was obvious.

"You get out of here!" Joseph shouted at him. "You have

NO right to be here!"

Kael lunged at him and slammed him against the nearest wall. "If you EVER touch Katherine or Gwyn again, I will make you suffer. . . and *believe* me. I know how to make humans suffer."

Joseph didn't know what to say. He wanted to make some sort of threat, but Kael was going to win this argument either way. Aliens put the fear of God into him. Kael knew that which was why he knew that Joseph would stop trying to intimidate women with violence. Kael was all about saving humans. But Joseph had hurt his poor wife, who loved him anyway. Joseph didn't count as human. He wasn't worth saving.

Attempting to calm himself down, Kael knelt beside his former fiancé. "Gwyn. . . love of my life. . . I don't know what they said to you, but I'm here. I'm not dead, alright? I'm right here in front of you. . . and I'm alive. So it's okay now. I'm not going anywhere." He did have to admit that he was relieved. It meant that she still loved him. Her reaction proved it. He didn't know why she believed Ana, but he was almost glad that she did.

It didn't take long for her to recognize his voice. She sat there for a few minutes and let herself relax and soak in the fact that he was still alive. When she fully came out of her daze, she got to her feet with Kael's help. "Thanks." She couldn't think of what to say to him. He could come to her rescue, but she thought he was dead. "Can we have a few minutes alone?"

Allison, Joseph and Katherine stepped out of the room and Kael closed the door. "Ana said that your parents helped her. They must've come to her with the idea. . . not that she wouldn't have thought of it on her own."

"I know I shouldn't have believed her, Kael," she said quietly. "Deep down, I always feared that something would happen to you. I always thought there would be that heartbreaking moment when you would be taken away from me. . . I guess I just thought that was it."

"I wasn't taken away from you, Gwyn. We chose to separate from each other. Not willingly, but that was what you wanted."

"I know," she nodded solemnly, "I know." There was a long pause before she spoke again. "You look good. I mean, you look like you're doing well."

"I guess I am. . ."

"So why are you doing so well when I'm not?"

This was going to be difficult. He'd gotten so good at lying that he had he would be able to pull this off. He just didn't want to. "I let you go. I had to. I wouldn't be able to focus otherwise. I want you to be okay too. I want you to be able to move on with your life."

"I think I can do that. It'd be better for both of us to remain apart."

Kael nodded. "Good. . . well. . . that's it then." He wanted to touch her hand or give her a kiss on the cheek. In all honesty, he wanted to do a hell of a lot more than that, but for Gwyn's sake, he would control himself. "It was good to see you."

She forced a smile and waited for him to disappear. He'd probably gone back to his ship. To Ana. To his family. Who knew if he had friends. She wondered what he did there. Was he torturing and killing humans again? Was he pleading her case to his parents? She doubted that she would ever know. One thing she *did* know was that she missed him.

Kael did go back to Ana. She was fast asleep by now and he wasn't going to wake her up and give her a lecture. He was going to let it go. As long as Gwyn wasn't physically hurt, he would have to deal with it. Though he would be miserable without her, it really was best for them to stay as they were. Apart and not together. . . separate and alone.

***

Months went by though no one noticed. They were so busy with their lives. Gwyn had negotiated with the aliens. Now they knew exactly when and where the battle would be. A contract was signed as well. Gwyn had faith that they would be true to their word. But just in case, there were going to be troops all over the United States, ready to fight. It had been agreed that the battle would remain tidy and civilized. Attacks wouldn't be unorganized and all over the country.

Again, Gwyn believed that they would keep their word, but she wasn't gullible. She was ready for anything. She had been training her own troops and preparing them for what was ahead. She had decided to become the leader of the army, or one of them, anyway.

Kael had been roaming around hunting down his kind if they should attempt to harm any humans. He had saved a lot of lives. It was amazing how blood-thirsty they seemed to be, even with the battle approaching. It wasn't fair for them to be killing humans for fun. Kael just wouldn't put up with it anymore. Along with being a hero in his spare time, he was still pretending to be in love with Ana.

He was doing all of this saving lives business under the radar. He had to be careful. His people may not be watching him, but they would certainly turn their heads if he ended up on the television or in a newspaper. He was heroic, not stupid.

Gwyn was at a bar with a few of the troops from her army enjoying a few drinks and relaxing after a long day. They often went weeks without a single break. They woke up, choked down breakfast and trained. Then they choked down lunch and trained. By dinner, they were famished and ate faster than they should. . . then they trained again. After that, they went to bed. It was nice to go out for a good time when they could.

Gwyn sipped her drink and nodded her head to the rhythm of the music. She was scanning the room and still performing her daily duties. It was a habit now. She couldn't help it. She felt like a mama bear around the young men and women she was training.

Kael came into the bar and shook off the fight he'd just had. He knew he was dirty and must have looked rough, but no one looked up at him – except for Gwyn. That was the norm for a lot of people these days-walking around with blood or goo on them.

He stood next to Gwyn at the bar and ordered himself a drink; a smile was gracing his lips. It had been a while since he'd smiled. "Hey, you."

Gwyn smiled back. "Are you okay?"

"Oh, yeah." He wiped a bit of green goop from his shoulder. "I was in a fight. I won, of course."

"Is the goop yours?"

"Thankfully, no. When we look like humans, we bleed red blood, same as you. When we're in our true form, we bleed multicolored goop."

"That's pretty gross," she giggled.

"You haven't spilled extraterrestrial blood, then?"

"No, not yet. We don't go looking for fights. . . unlike you, apparently. We're saving it all up for the big day."

Kael nodded and sipped his drink. "So you haven't been attacked by random aliens?"

"Nope. It's weird how they're everywhere these days. Most of the ones I've encountered are friendly. Some are violent. But they seem to be saving up their energy as well."

"Well, I want you to be careful. The big day is drawing nearer and they may get anxious. Promise me you'll watch your back."

"I always do." She tilted her head, her eyes wandering over him slowly. There was something about him. She couldn't look away from him. "Do you want to go outside?"

"Yeah, sure."

Gwyn told her troops that she was off for the night and went outside with Kael. They stood outside the bar enjoying the cool summer breeze.

"Is your uniform *supposed* to be sexy?" He looked up at the stars for a moment before looking back at her.

"Why? Is it?" He nodded and she grinned. She felt like she had in the beginning with him. Nothing was complicated. They were just in love. They didn't have to be anything else. "You're different."

"So are you." He wanted to scoop her up in his arms and take her as far away from here as possible. He didn't want to deal with the violence that awaited them. He wanted to soak in her, for she was his sun. "I feel good. I know I have a purpose and I know I'm *doing* good. It's a great feeling. . . to be important, I suppose. To be a part of something bigger."

Gwyn nodded. "I feel the same way." At this moment in time, she didn't *want* to be a part of something bigger. She wanted to be a normal person and have a normal life. He seemed to bring that out in her. "Maybe I can put in a good word for you. I'd like you to see what I do now."

"I'd like that." This wasn't good. She was like a drug. Now that he was near her, he didn't want to leave. He would have to tear himself away from her before he got all mushy and professed his undying love. Neither of them needed that. "Well, I'm glad we're both doing well."

These past months felt like a lie. They felt like a front. Why did he have to come to her? Why couldn't he just stay away? This was ridiculous. Her feelings for him were resurfacing. "Are we?"

Kael breathed a soft sigh. "I won't lie. It's not the same without you."

"And vice versa. But I think it'd be too difficult, especially now."

"You're right. It's probably better for us to stay apart at this point. We don't need to complicate things this late in the game."

"Good." There was an uncomfortable silence. They were both making excuses, but it was the best thing to do. "So. . . maybe I'll see you around?"

"I certainly hope so." As he watched her walk away, his heart sank. He wanted to follow her. He wanted to walk beside her. *Anything* but watch her walk away from him.

Kael went grudgingly back to the ship and into his room;

he sat down on the bed next to Ana. She was eating something that looked like a human hand. . . and it probably was. "Can you not do that in front of me?"

"What? Eat?" She turned up the television once she realized it was praising her murderous deeds that day.

"No, eat *that*. You know I think it's repulsive."

"If you don't care about the humans anymore, you shouldn't care if I eat them or not. Besides, the guy's dead. It's not like he cares."

Kael rolled his eyes. He couldn't help but see Gwyn's face attached to the hand Ana was eating. What if - one day - Ana was consuming Gwyn's body? He wouldn't know until it was too late.

"I want to talk about the wedding," she said.

"Whose wedding?"

"*Ours*, you idiot."

"I don't want to talk about it. I hate weddings. I've hated them since I was a child."

"Ah, that's only because you thought you'd never get married!" She set down her food and tried to give him a kiss, but he shoved her away.

"You look disgusting today. I won't even *consider* talking about marriage until you look something close to irresistible," he paused and looked her over, "And you have a long way to go, my pet."

"Ooh, I like it when you're mean." He could have said worse things to her, and she loved him so he didn't mind his insults. "You know, there was a time when you thought the stench of death smelled like flowers on my skin."

"Things change, Ana. Some days I can tolerate you, and some days I can't. Today, I can't. I'm not in the mood."

"What's the matter?"

He had to give her some sort of excuse. "A human got the better of me. I was overcome, overwhelmed. I didn't know what to do. This human made me feel so degraded. It crept into every fiber of my being and filled me with emotion. It's still in my system. . . throwing me off." Hey, it wasn't a lie.

She wrapped her arms around him. "This human sounds awful. A warlock, perhaps. . . if those still exist. Did you kill it?"

Now the lie. "I shredded it to pieces. . . and I still managed to look pleasing to the eye while doing so."

"Oh, I'll go change into a sundress if that'll make you happy."

Kael smirked and threw her off of the bed. "Or you can skip the changing part and just get naked." Ana loved the sound of that and he hated it. He deserved an Oscar for this. . . or at least a Golden Globe.

Gwyn was sitting in the kitchen with Allison as usual. She had to fill her in. "I'm. . . awestruck. I can't believe how much he's changed." Her skin was practically glowing. She knew that her aura was.

"Yeah. . . apparently." Allison sipped her coffee, wondering if Gwyn would ever stop talking about Kael. "You have stars in your eyes."

She sighed heavily. She knew that she did. She couldn't deny that she was still in love. "I can't say that I don't want him back. But we've agreed not to go there. It wouldn't work out. It's all. . . too. . . complicated."

"Yeah, well, you say that *now*. Life changes every day. You never know what it'll toss at you next. Be prepared for complications."

It was only half an hour later when they heard something upstairs. It sounded like something hitting the floor. Fearing the worst, the two of them rushed upstairs to Johnny's room.

When they opened the door, they were surprised to find Kael there. He and Johnny seemed to be having a tickle war.

"Hi, guys," Allison said.

Thinking he must be in trouble Johnny sprung up from the floor. "Ummm. . . hi, mom."

"Johnny, I give you permission to stay up late tonight. Let's go watch a movie, okay?" Johnny nodded eagerly and followed his mother downstairs - after Allison had given Gwyn raised eyebrows.

Kael got up off of the floor, cleared his throat, and stood awkwardly in front of her. "I hope this isn't a problem. We were just goofing off. The kid looked lonely, so I thought I'd pay him a visit."

"You don't have to explain yourself," Gwyn smiled, "It's good that you're still seeing him. He misses you. You're the only father figure he has. . ."

Kael nodded. He did understand that. He just hoped that he would be in their lives for a very long time. "Right. . ."

Fearing another awkward silence, she spoke again. "I talked to Allison. . . I told her that I saw you earlier. I think she's tired of listening to me talk about you."

"Oh, yeah?" His ears perked up and his voice became a little higher. He was excited that she was talking about him. "What'd you say?"

"I. . . couldn't say that I didn't want to be with you."

Another smile. A *real* smile. A happy one. "That's. . . I'm very glad to hear that." She smiled back at him and his whole word seemed brighter. Not even Ana could bring him down. Speaking of. . . "I should get going. I kind of snuck out, so. . ."

"Yeah, right. I guess I'll see you soon. . . I hope."

***

Gwyn was out to dinner with her parents. They were both very quiet. It probably had something to do with Kael giving her father a wake-up call. Their silence didn't bother her. She had a distraction; she couldn't stop thinking about Kael. She wondered if they would freak out if she mentioned him.

"So I. . . saw Kael again."

Katherine merely looked up at her. Joseph dropped his fork. "You. . . saw him?"

"Yes," she nodded, "We talked. It was really nice. It was like. . . I was an unsolved puzzle. . . and he was my missing piece."

"Do you really feel that way about him?" Katherine asked.

"I do. I never stopped loving him."

"He's still an alien," Joseph struggled to keep his voice steady, "He betrayed you. He betrayed your country."

"Gwyn's an adult, Joseph," Katherine spoke softly, "She knows what he's done and it seems that she loves him despite his faults. It's her decision - not ours."

There was a long pause before he grumbled, "You're right."

Gwyn almost fell out of her chair. Her father never admitted to be wrong. He had quite the temper and it must have killed him not to raise his voice to them, but he was changing too. It was just another way that Kael had bettered her life.

Later that night, Kael was out and about. Ana was busy planning the wedding and she had shooed him off so that she could work. Now *he* could work. It was difficult to get away from her and save lives.

He could sense an alien nearby. It didn't feel harmless. It felt hostile. He followed his senses and they led him to a house. He could hear the screams from outside, so he hurried through the door.

The alien was in its true form. Whatever species it was, it was ugly. It looked like it had jumped out of a nightmare. Its eyes were yellow and its skin was scaly and green. Its face was similar to an alligator, but it was round like a human's. The rest of its skin was covered in a leather suit of some kind.

There was a mother huddled against the wall with her two children, the father stood in front of them in an effort to be their shield. Kael came at the alien and tried to pull him away from the family. The alien was strong and it sent him flying into a wall.

Kael jumped back on his feet, clenched his fists and threw punches at the alien's face. It seemed to be its weakness. The suit it was wearing might be impenetrable, so he stuck at the face. If this stupid thing would just take a breather, he would be able to grab a weapon. The bad thing about saving lives was that he didn't have help. He couldn't sneak weapons without Ana noticing.

When he paused to look for a sharp object, the alien went for the family again. "Get out of here!" Kael yelled at them. They were too frightened to move and he understood that, but it would have been nice to have their cooperation.

He grabbed what little hair the alien had and threw him to the other side of them room, hoping it would give the family enough time to make a run for it. The mother took the hands of her children and headed for the door.

The alien suddenly appeared in front of them. Its hand drew back, but before it could strike them, the father raced in front of them. The alien made one swift movement across the father's neck. . . and it severed his head. The mother shrieked with grief and covered her children's eyes.

Kael roared with anger, kicking and grabbing the alien's ankles. He pulled on them, forcing it to the floor. He didn't give it time to react. He punched through the creature's head, knowing that it wasn't the prettiest sight, but it was effective. The alien was dead.

The widow clung to her children, sobbing as she looked up at him. There was nothing he could say that would make this better. Her husband was dead. She and her children had just been traumatized and their lives would never be the same. "I'm. . . so sorry for your loss."

Unable to think clearly, he left the house. He continued on his way, breathing heavily with pain and frustration. That man shouldn't have died. Kael should have moved faster – he should have done something more.

Gwyn was out with some of her troops. Three of them were girls and two of them were guys. They should have expected trouble. They should have been prepared. But they weren't.

Three aliens stormed in. They were holding what looked like very expensive squirt guns. She knew that they were designed to kill quickly, so she had to act fast. "Guys, find weapons!"

The aliens had the build of humans, but their skin was pink and their veins were purple. They didn't have hair on their skin; they were completely bald. Their eyes were small, beady and black.

All they could manage for weapons were knives, forks, and pool sticks. The government wouldn't allow the weapons they had designed to be taken off the army base. It didn't make sense now when they were fighting for their lives. It made Gwyn angry, but she didn't have time to think about it.

Her five troops tried to take on the three aliens. They were thrown all over the bar while Gwyn thought of a way to kill these things. She had to wait for the right time to strike. She had to hit them in the right places. They didn't have much to work with.

The pool stick wouldn't be strong enough to penetrate their skin. She broke one in half, hoping to make it easier to do more damage. As her troops fought and distracted them, she lunged at one of the aliens and drove the end of her pool stick into its throat. This made it bleed purple liquid, so she took it as a good sign. She knew she would have to stab it another time or two before it died.

She had to wait for another chance. She didn't get one before one of the aliens punched a hole through one of her female colleagues. The alien was distracted by killing the woman and Gwyn was able to stab it several times in the neck. It withdrew its fist from the female and dropped to the floor. The other two aliens - one of them seriously injured - left the bar. Gwyn was relieved. She wasn't sure that the others would have survived if they had stayed.

She showed no emotion as she watched the troops gather around their friend and grieve. She simply walked over to the phone and called the young woman's parents, informing them of her death. She then called the army base, also informing them, and then she left the bar. She knew the others would stay there until the body was taken away. She couldn't bear to sit there and stare at the blood, knowing how unprepared she had been.

Would it be like that at the battle? They would have weapons which would up their chances of survival. . . but would it make that much of a difference? Did they stand a chance? Was it really worth it? She was doubting everything as she walked all the way back to her house. When she walked in the door, she was greeted by Allison and Johnny.

"Kael's upstairs in your room," Allison said.

"Oh. . . he is?" She hadn't expected to see him so soon.

"Yeah!" Johnny said excitedly. "I think he's waiting for you."

"He looks pretty rough," Allison tilted her head at her cousin, "Kind of like you do."

"Yeah, okay." Gwyn closed the door and headed up the stairs. "I'll talk to you guys in the morning."

She took a deep breath and entered her bedroom, wishing she could change. But Kael didn't look any better than she did. She figured it was alright to look like crap if he did.

He was seated on her bed with his head in his hands. He looked up at her when he heard her come in; he was happy to see her and disappointed with himself that he had come here. "I'm sorry. . . I didn't know where else to go. I knew you would understand."

She sat down beside him and placed a gentle hand on his shoulder. "What happened?"

"I rescued a family tonight," he said lowly, "I followed the scent. . . I walked in on an alien about to slaughter a couple and their two children. I killed it. . . but it killed the man first. The way his wife screamed. . . " He shook his head with sorrow. "It was the most horrible sound I've ever heard."

"My heart made that sound when I thought I'd lost *you*," she said softly.

He leaned against her feeling content to be in her presence. "What about you? You look a bit out of sorts."

"I lost one of my troops. A few aliens crashed our party and. . . we were unarmed. We're not allowed to take our specially designed weapons, you see."

"I'm sorry. That had to be difficult."

"She was young. I kind of feel like. . . I'm responsible for them, you know? Like I'm their second mother. I've spent a lot of time with them. I've taught them."

"I know you have. And you know that you can't blame yourself. It isn't your fault that you were defenseless."

She would have argued, but she would lose. She thought it best to change the subject instead. "Did you *really* let me go?"

What a question. He didn't think that she would ever ask, so he wasn't prepared to answer. "You want to know the truth?"

She nodded. "Always."

"It was a load of crap." They both would have laughed if they hadn't looked so serious. "I still love you. . . always will. It's as simple as that."

"Then I. . . have to confess that I was going back to you." She nuzzled his shoulder. "I thought it over and knew that there was nothing more important than being with you. That's when I went to your house and Ana told me that you had died. She said that you had died from complications of your torture."

"I wanted to give up. I really did. If we're being honest, my anger was what kept me going. Then *I* thought everything over and realized that I could do a lot of good. I could redeem myself. . . I'm still working on that part."

"I believe in you." Against her better judgment, she sat up and pressed her lips to his.

He wanted to take it further, but he knew she wasn't ready yet. So when he was finally able to tear himself away, he began to stroke her hair. "I'm still baffled. I was so terrible for so long. I don't understand how I'm capable of being so in love with you."

She smiled. "Will you come visit me at the army base? You could meet me there and maybe we could. . . go out. . . on a date?"

"Are you sure they'll let me in?"

"You can just meet me outside. It'll make it easier."

"Okay, then. I'll stop by tomorrow." Knowing that he had to if he was going to contain his happiness, he gently kissed her forehead and disappeared.

He appeared back in his bedroom where Ana greeted him with a tight hug. "Where do you go when you're not with me?"

Because of how tightly she hugged him, he assumed that she knew what he had been doing. "I'm just getting to know my way around the battlefield. . ."

"You're not screwing someone else?"

Kael coughed and stepped back from her. "No, Ana. I'm not having an affair. Why do you ask?"

"Well, I want to talk to you about something."

"Uh. . . okay."

She sat him down on their bed and took his hand in hers. "I want us to. . . try for a baby."

That was one of the worst things she could have said. Gwyn was the only woman he wanted to have children with. "I'm not sure that's the best thing right now."

Ana pouted her lip. "Why not?"

"Do *you* really think it's the best thing for us to be trying for a baby with the battle so near?"

She sighed exasperatedly. "I guess you're right. I just. . . I really want to have a family with you. We're already engaged, so it's only natural, right?"

"Yes. . . and I promise that we'll discuss a family when all of this is over."

***

Gwyn had finished her training for the day and was now waiting for Kael. She hoped that no one suspected who she was going to meet with. It might get them both into a lot of trouble. Come to think of it, she didn't know why she suggested that they meet there. She could have just told him to meet her at her house. Maybe she — subconsciously — wanted them to be seen.

She was relieved when he arrived. "It's about time. I've been waiting for half an hour."

"Well, Ana wouldn't let me get away," he gave her a kiss on the cheek, "She might suspect something."

"I don't think she's the only one. Let's get out of here before someone sees us. This was a bad idea."

He took her hand, and they disappeared from the base; they reappeared in her kitchen. It was a nifty ability. "Do you want to get into something more comfortable?"

She raised an eyebrow. "Is this your way of trying to seduce me?"

He chuckled. "No. Not that I wouldn't love to."

She shook her head, went upstairs, and changed into a t-shirt and sweatpants. Then she went back into the kitchen and started to make their dinner.

"You look like you were meant to wear that army uniform," he said.

"You think so? I don't." She threw a bit of salt into a pot of water. "I feel like I'm lying when I wear it. It's not who I am."

"Yes it is." He sat at the table and watched her as she

cooked. "It's just not *all* that you are."

"You have a way of making perfect sense." Something was bothering her and he knew it. She had a *thinking* look on her face. He just hoped that it wouldn't tear them apart again.

They were silent until the pasta was ready. Then she served it and sat down across from him. "So how have you been?"

"Ana wants to get married," he shook his head and stabbed his noodles with his fork, "We talked about having a baby last night. We're actually secretly engaged right now."

"Are you happy with Ana?" she asked curiously.

He almost choked on his food. "Hell no."

"It was just a question. . ."

"Gwyn," he reached across the table and took her hand, "Don't you know that you are the *only* woman I see when I look into my future?"

"Well, you also once said that I was the only woman you ever wanted to be with, and you slept with Ana a number of times. . . still *are*, if I'm not mistaken."

"That's different. *We're* different. . . and I'm only sleeping with her because I have to. Think of me as an undercover cop. It's part of my cover."

"But you do want those things? Marriage. . . children. . ."

"Yeah, of course. But not with Ana."

"I guess that's good. I've been thinking about those things too. . ."

That made him happy. There was something else that she wanted to bring up, so he was waiting for her to. Once their plates were clean, they went up to her bedroom.

They sat down on her bed and stared at each other for a while. That was fun. . . if awkwardness *could* be fun. It was a good half hour before either one of them said anything.

"I, um. . . I'm scared," Gwyn confessed. She hadn't wanted to say anything. She didn't want to jinx them or something. She was still confused as tiring as that may seem to everyone else.

"I figured you might be. You were so quiet." He knew that she was being hesitant for a reason. "I'm scared too. I don't know what's going to happen. But I want you to be prepared, alright?"

She was having a case of déjà vu. He was talking as if they would never see each other again. "Okay."

"I've made you a list," he pulled out a piece of paper from one of his pockets, "We've built new shields to block blasts of energy from your new weapons. So this is a list of everything new that they have. . . and their plans so far."

Gwyn took the piece of paper and tucked in safely in her

dresser. "Kael. . . I want you to fight with us."

So, it was out. What he sensed had been bothering her. "Gwyn. . . you know I can't do that. I have to start out with their army at least. As soon as the battle starts, you *know* I'll be on your side."

"I don't care about that. I want you at *my* side. . ."

"I wish I could be, my love. You know I do. You also know that it would be better for me to stay put. If I join you now, Ana will kill you for sure. At least on the battlefield, I have a shot at seeing you alive again."

Gwyn was getting frustrated. To her, at this moment, it all sounded like excuses. She reminded herself that she had to be careful. She had to think of people; someone other than herself. "How do I know you won't betray us? You've lied to me before."

"Damn it, Gwyn." He rose from the bed, his fists clenching and unclenching. "You're doing it again. You're pushing me away. This isn't about them. It's about *you*, it's about *us*. You're afraid, and you're hiding behind anything you can."

God, it was so true-all of it. But, she was stubborn. She had her mind made up, and she wasn't going to let him talk her out of this. "If that's how you feel, then I think you should leave."

He knew that was coming. How could he not? "Every time you feel too much. . . every time this feels too real. . . you push me away. You run. Maybe because you feel

177

guilty. Maybe because you don't want to trust me with your heart. Honestly, after what my family put you through, I understand. I do. But it's not right to make me believe that I *am* what you want."

She had to hold back her tears. She wanted him more than anything, but she had a world to protect. Her expression was stiff and her eyes were cold. "I believe I asked you to leave."

Kael let out a slow breath. His heart was breaking. He didn't want it to end like this. What if one of them died? What if they *both* died? All he could do was hope that they would see each other again. "I wish you would let me love you."

With that, he vanished from her bedroom and reappeared in his own. Ana was there. It wasn't exactly a surprise. She practically lived with him now.

She had a very smug smirk on her face, as if she knew what had happened. . . and maybe she did. "You were with *her*, weren't you?"

Kael blinked back his tears and nodded awkwardly. "Yes."

Ana giggled. His misfortune was her amusement. She had known for quite some time that Kael was off with Gwyn, professing his love, possibly screwing her. . . that wasn't as awful as the lying. Ana *hated* the lies. "Gwyn can't handle you. She doesn't know how."

"And *you* do?"

"Yes, my disloyal pet. *I* am the one who really loves you. I don't try to change you. I love you for who you are." She pressed her body against his and twisted her fingers in his hair.

Kael shoved her away from him. There was no sense in hiding his hatred for her. "No, Ana. You love me for who I *was*. That man doesn't exist anymore."

"You're not a man, Kael."

Kael rolled his eyes, opened his door, and gestured for her to get out. "The best part about you knowing the truth is that I don't have to pretend to love you a second longer."

His words stung, but she held her smirk as she walked out the door. She could run off to his parents and tell them all about Kael's betrayal. He would die. Gwyn would probably die as well.

She *could* do that. . . but she wanted to have the satisfaction of killing Gwyn herself. She was planning her revenge.

***

It was the day of the battle. The sky was grey as if it knew what was going to happen. Today was not a day for sunshine. Gwyn was saying her goodbyes. She didn't know if she would be back. She was hopeful, of course, but unsure. She was just happy to know that Allison and Johnny would be okay.

"A car will be here soon," she said as she stood at the door, "You'll be taken to a safe place."

"When will we see you again?" Johnny asked.

Allison wasn't going to show her concern in front of her son. He was a child. He wasn't completely clueless and he knew the seriousness of all of this, but she wasn't going to tell him that Gwyn might not come back. "We don't know yet, honey. It might be tomorrow; it might be a few days."

"Everything will be alright," Gwyn told him, "We'll see each other soon. I promise." She gave them both a tight hug and only looked back once at Allison. Neither of them had to speak; they were saying farewell with their eyes. There was nothing they could say to sum up their relationship. They had become each other's best friends.

Her heart would give out if she stayed much longer, so she waved to them and was out the door. She was taken to the base first. The troops were ready to fight, and their weapons were with them. Gwyn had checked over Kael's list a thousand times. It hadn't taken long to adjust their weapons. . . she had just wanted to look at his hand-writing.

She didn't want to admit it to herself, but she missed him. She wanted to be with him today of all days. A part of her hoped that he would stand by what he said. He'd told her that the royal families let others do the fighting for them. With any luck, he would sit this one out. With any luck, she would survive and see him again.

As she stood at the battlefield, he was all she could think about. Half of the land was empty; the aliens would arrive on that side. The grass was freshly cut-not that that mattered. It was very green though the fog that was filling the air gave it an almost muddy look. She hoped that the fog wouldn't be too heavy. It would be a great disadvantage to the humans.

She was thinking about so many things at this moment. She wondered if she would see her family again. She figured that she would, one way or another. If she lived, she would get to see Allison, Johnny, and her parents. If she died, she would get to see her brothers and sisters. God, her siblings. . . what did *they* think of all this?

She shouldn't have told Kael to leave. She didn't care who he was, what he was, or what he had done. She loved him and all that he was. She wasn't angry at him. She never really had been. He knew her better than she knew herself. She needed to tell him that. He needed to know that she was sorry. . . he needed to know that she loved him.

She only closed her eyes for a second. When she opened them, there was a circular ship hovering above them. It was so large. She didn't like the sound; it was like being on an airplane- only ten times worse. Her ears hurt. It was going to be hard to focus.

After a moment, the sound stopped. She was grateful for that; but she knew what was coming next, and she wished she didn't. "They're here."

They appeared on the other side of the field. They reminded her of a rainbow. They were all sorts of colors. Some of them looked human, but most of them were a variety of colors. . . blue, pink, purple, green, and even yellow. She was watching for Kael, but there was no way she would be able to see him.

Kael and Ana were standing next to each other; both were in the middle of the army. He thought that might be best. He would be able to work from the inside out. He wasn't being conceited either. He knew that he was a skilled fighter. It used to be his passion as a matter of fact. Fighting. . . killing. . . they used to be his reasons to live-that, and Ana. But that had all changed.

Ana's only thought was her revenge. As much as she hated to miss something like this, she was going to leave early. There was something a little more important. It wouldn't take long, and she hated that as well. It would be short and quick. Then she would return to the fight with a satisfied grin.

There was a long silence as they all stared at each other. Gwyn could feel some of the troops quivering beside her. It made her feel horrible. She wished that none of this was happening. She wanted it all to go away. She wanted to send these people home and tell them that this was all a mistake, that aliens weren't real. . . just a figment of their imaginations. She couldn't do that. It wasn't possible.

She didn't think that the fight would ever begin because no one was moving. After what seemed like hours, one of the quivering troops pulled back the trigger of their specially designed gun. A burst of blue energy came from the weapon and liquefied an alien. A cry from somewhere was heard and it announced what they all knew. It had begun.

Allison was sitting with Johnny near the front door. They were still at Gwyn's house. She didn't want to show how worried she was. But the car hadn't come for them yet. . . and she was starting to think that it wasn't *going* to come. "Mommy, why aren't they here yet?" Johnny knew she was worried. He knew because of how tightly she was hugging him.

"I don't know, sweetie. I think we should get out of the living room though. Come on."

She quickly went into the kitchen and grabbed them some food and water. Then she took him into the basement and left the door cracked open, just in case people did come for them. She was hoping that they were just late.

Johnny watched his mother as she came down the stairs not wanting to tell her that he knew exactly what was going on. "I'm scared. . ."

"Oh, don't be. . . we'll be fine. I don't think anyone will bother us."

He nodded and walked over to a dusty bookshelf thankful that there were some children's books there. They would comfort him. "Could you read to me?"

Allison smiled cheerfully. "Of course."

Both sides were mingled now. It was hard to tell who was who except for those who were kind enough to be there without their transmitters. Gwyn's worst fear was that she would kill someone who was on her side. Kael was a different story. She knew him intimately. She hadn't seen a lot of the men and women who were in her army very often, so she might kill one of them and not know it.

Kael was slaughtering his own and quite happily at that. He switched from his guns to his swords blasting and slicing anyone he could. There wasn't an ounce of guilt in him as he split their multi-colored blood. He knew what they were capable of.

They were like him except that they hadn't changed their ways, and they would probably continue them for the rest of their lives.

He could sense Gwyn on the field. She was there somewhere and he needed to get to her. He wanted to protect her as much as he could before he was done for – he was sure that *someone* would spill his blood if not Ana.

Gwyn could barely focus. She watched some aliens liquefy while others shrieked and bled until they drew their last breaths. She saw Kael in every one of them. That was why she couldn't focus. She was also worried about everything that she shouldn't be. She was worried about Allison and Johnny. She was worried about her troops. She *had* to keep her mind off of all that. If she wasn't careful, she would end up dying a hell of a lot sooner than she wanted to.

Ana was enjoying slaughtering humans more than Kael was enjoying slaughtering aliens. She loved the way they cried out when she stabbed or punched holes through them. She was covered in their blood-red, sticky, and thick. It was disgusting but also liberating. It was too bad that she had to sneak away. She couldn't decide what she loved to do more--killing people or causing misery. Kael was going to regret all his promises. . . all his lies.

Allison was still reading to Johnny even though he had fallen asleep. She knew that something terrible was going to happen. Her only wish was to be able to protect her son.

She wanted a weapon. She should have asked Gwyn for one, but she had trusted the president. He'd promised that they would be safe and away from the battle. Either he was lying, or he was dead. Maybe both.

As she had suspected and feared, Ana trotted down the basement steps. Allison hugged Johnny tightly to her and prayed for her son's life to be spared. "What do you want?"

Ana sniffed the air. It smelled so clean compared to where she had just been. "I'm sick of Kael thinking that he can betray me and get away with it. I'm going to show him who's better."

It didn't matter what she said. She knew that their lives were over. She was only grateful that Johnny was asleep; his death would be peaceful. "Kael is a better being than you could ever *hope* to be."

Ana shrugged not really caring of the opinion of a human. "Are you going to beg?"

Allison shook her head. "Not for my life. . . for my son's. He's innocent in all of this."

"No, I'm afraid he isn't. Kael's become attached to this boy. Besides, I have to make up for all the humans that he spared, don't I?"

Allison's eyes filled with tears. "Well. . . it was worth a try."

Ana couldn't show mercy to these things. She imagined that if *she* ever had a child, she would do anything to keep it alive. . . even beg. Humans didn't count though. Not in her eyes. They all deserved to die.

So many people were dead. Gwyn wanted to collapse from the sick feeling in her stomach, but she forced herself to keep going. If she fell once, she wouldn't rise again. That was all it would take-one flinch, one mistake.

She thought that the battle would only last a few minutes and that the aliens would win. Her troops were putting up a good fight. They were doing well, and she was proud of them. Some humans – and even aliens – lasted longer than others. . . and all of them looked too young to die.

Ana appeared in a flash before her. Just as she knew she would, she had a very wide and satisfied grin on her face. She couldn't wait to tell Gwyn what she had done. "You look tired, sweetie. Do you need a breather before I kill you?"

She was *extremely* tired. But Ana had a way of lighting a fire inside of her. She was ready to fight the thing that had caused so much grief for her. She was ready to die too. "Has anyone ever told you that you talk too much?"

"I only spoke two sentences."

"You're still talking."

This wouldn't be settled with blasts of whatever. This was worthy of her sword. She threw away the gun that would easily take Ana's life and pulled out her sword instead swinging at her in anger.

Liza was combing her hair with her fingers pacing worriedly in her parents dining room. They were enjoying a hearty meal while their son and so many others were fighting for their lives.

"Calm yourself," Gavin told her, "There's nothing to worry about."

"You don't understand," Liza said heatedly, "You have no compassion for anyone but yourselves."

"That's not true," Leah insisted, "I'm worried about Kael and Ana. We know perfectly well that they may lose their lives. This is quite serious."

"I know it is! Yet, you sit there, perfectly calm and collected. What if Kael does? What if Ana kills him?"

"We trust Ana with our lives," Gavin nodded matter-of-factly.

"Therein lies the problem. People are dying for YOUR selfish reasons."

Leah rolled her eyes. "You sound like your brother, Liza. This doesn't concern you. There's nothing you can do about it, so why don't you sit down and eat with us?"

Liza wanted to stomp her feet like a child. They weren't listening to her - not that they ever did. If something happened to Kael, she hoped that it would make them see the consequences of their actions. There was no need for this violence. She didn't understand why they couldn't all get along as juvenile as that may sound.

Kael crouched to his feet and sprung back up ducking as a blade tried to separate his head from his body.

He stabbed the alien quickly and blocked out the rest of the battle; his eyes were focused on two people. Ana and Gwyn were at each other's throats – not literally, but their swords were thrusting at each other wildly. Neither of them could get in a good blow. Each swing was blocked, and each attack to end one another's lives failed.

He didn't mind that part of it. He was rooting for Gwyn to win of course. He knew Ana's techniques and knew that she was strong and skilled, but so was Gwyn. She did have a chance. He had to remind himself of that. Still, he wanted to get to them. He might be able to stop Ana before Gwyn was seriously injured.

His breath suddenly hitched in his chest. He knew it was a bad idea to let his guard down. It was incredibly stupid of him. He was fighting mechanically as if he'd been programmed to dodge attacks and kill anyone lunging at him. Other than the fact that not paying attention to his surroundings was the worst idea in the world, he couldn't protect himself from attacks that came from behind.

Kael fell to his knees; the white hot pain surged through

his veins. *Why* had they designed these things for a painful death? He could have told Gwyn to make it quick and simple, but he hadn't. He had told her to make it as painful as possible. . . and it truly was. He had felt worse pain; he had to admit. It didn't help that he knew his life was ending. The sword had entered from his back, went through his body, and stuck out of his gut. *That* was painful. He was waiting for his head to be chopped off next.

It was luck that whoever had stabbed him withdrew the sword and went on to the next victim. Kael forced himself to stand and felt how weak his body had already become. It hurt to move. It hurt to breathe. But there was work to be done. He had to try to get to Gwyn. Even if he failed. . . he had to try.

It was funny how his transmitter not only made him *look* human, but it made him *feel* human. He could feel the blood swimming around his wound as well as escaping it. He didn't want to look down. He didn't want to see how bad it was.

The pain was dull enough for him to continue walking. It was more of an ache. His vision was starting to blur, and it was much too soon for that. It wasn't over yet. Not until he saw her. Not until he knew what would happen to her. He couldn't be at peace without dying in her arms. If he had to choose how he died, dying in the arms of the woman he loved didn't sound half as heartbreaking as it would look.

"I knew it would end this way," Ana said breathlessly, "I

knew that I would kill you. I've known since the day we met."

"Stop talking." Gwyn was here to kill Ana or die trying – not take a stroll down memory lane. Ana really was annoying.

"Why? You'll only die sooner." Ana smirked and lunged for Gwyn's shoulder. Gwyn blocked it. They weren't getting anywhere yet, but she knew that if she was patient, Gwyn would die. "You won't kill me. You don't have the guts."

"You're right." Gwyn pushed Ana's sword away with her own and lunged for her stomach which Ana blocked. "I'm not like you, Ana. I'm not a cold-blooded killer. That's why Kael loves me."

If ever there was a moment to shut Gwyn up, it was now – and she was going to take it. She came down with her sword aiming at Gwyn's throat. Gwyn blocked the attack and threw the sword away from her with such force that it flew into the air.

Ana wasn't worried. She drew a second sword that she had been able to keep hidden from Gwyn, and as she came at Ana for the final time, Ana drove the sword into her stomach.

Gwyn drew in a sharp breath. It wasn't that she had expected it; she had. She just thought that Ana would think of a more original way to kill her.

Ana blinked. She could feel Kael's pain and how extreme it

was. He was bleeding. . . he was dying. How could he be so stupid? How could *she*? She was so focused on killing Gwyn that she had forgotten about Kael. "I have been waiting for this day. . . for *so* long."

Gwyn pulled the sword from her body and pressed her hand against her wound. "How nice for you."

Ana chuckled sadly as her eyes filled with tears. She thought that it would feel better than it did. Maybe it didn't feel right because Kael was dying, and she hadn't planned on that. "They're dead, you know. . ."

She choked back a sob. She knew that Ana was referring to at least two of the three people she was most worried about today. "No. . ."

"I killed Allison first. She begged and begged for her son's life until I gutted her. The fear in her eyes. . . it was breath-taking."

Gwyn stared at the blood-stained grass. She didn't want to hear any of this.

"You should be grateful that I gave the boy such a quick death. He woke up when he heard his mother's screams. Then *he* started to scream, so I just stuck a sword in his heart. He didn't make a sound after that."

Tears trickled down Gwyn's cheeks. "You're a monster."

"Now, Kael. . . that was his own fault."

Gwyn looked up at her again. The one person she thought

would be alive after this. . .

"Yes, Gwyn. He's dying. It's your fault too. You're such a distraction to him."

Ana had nothing more to say to this pathetic human. She gritted her teeth and walked away from her continuing her slaughtering until she reached Kael.

She was surprised by how upset she was. "You deserved this, you know."

"I know." Kael was on the ground now. The pain had hit him. It was shear agony. He had to let himself rest or he would surely die before he found Gwyn. "Where is she?"

Ana pointed in the direction she last saw Gwyn. "Same as you."

His heart broke into pieces; it crumbled to the ground beneath him and turned into dust. She was dying. He had known this would happen. . . he had known. But it didn't make it any easier to hear. "Ana. . ."

"I don't want to hear anything you have to say." She knelt beside him and gave him a tearful kiss; their history was shining in her eyes. "We could have had something. We could have been the greatest warriors these two worlds have ever seen. We could have. . . raised a family."

"I'm sorry, Ana. I really am."

Ana tore herself from his side and returned to their ship. She would end up getting herself killed if she fought in this state.

Kael forced himself to his feet again sure that he would die before he managed to find Gwyn. He wandered through the fighting, the blood, and the bodies to find her at the edge of the field. She was supporting herself against a tree and staring into the distance. He felt great relief and despair when he saw her.

"Well," he said, "If we're going to die, I say we do so away from here."

She nodded and didn't argue as he helped her into the woods. They found a cabin far enough into the trees that they couldn't hear the noise from beyond. It was abandoned, but not old. In fact, it looked like the owners had simply fled most likely wanting to be nowhere near this place.

He sat her down by the fireplace; his eyes were blurring again-this time because of tears. The blood had soaked her stomach down to her thighs. He thought that he must have looked just as bad, if not worse. She didn't seem to be paying attention.

"Are you hungry?" he asked.

"No," she replied, "Just cold."

There was a stack of wood tucked in a corner, so he used that to make the best fire he could. He was cold too. It was hard work losing so much blood.

He laid by the fire and let her curl up in his arms. That was when she started to realize what was happening. She had been in a daze since she'd been stabbed. Now. . . she knew that they were dying. . . both of them. Kael seemed to have blood covering both sides of him. She didn't want to look closer for fear of losing consciousness. She had to stay awake for as long as she could.

"I'm sorry for starting a fight with you," she said, her voice was barely above a whisper.

"You always fight with me," he chuckled.

"It's because you always seemed too good to be true."

Kael wanted to laugh, but he knew that would probably hurt her as much as it would hurt him. "After all I've done, you think I'm too good to be true? I murdered your siblings. . . among many, *many* unspeakable things in my past."

Gwyn looked up at him. "I never see those things when I look at you."

"I'm glad," he sighed tearfully, "I was afraid that was *all* you could see. . . "

She shook her head. "No. . . and now we've run out of time."

"Well, we're together at the end. That's all that matters."

She smiled softly and rested her head against his chest. "Tell me how you fell in love with me. . . out of all others."

Kael closed his eyes. This would be the last thing he ever said to her. "I could. . . sense your existence. I've been able to feel you since the day I was born."

She smiled again, this time, closing her eyes. She knew that story, but she wanted to hear it one last time. "Really?"

He buried a sob deep within his chest; he wanted to sound strong for her. "I knew that you were out there somewhere. I just didn't know when you would come into my life. Instead of embracing it, I rebelled. I tried to escape it by doing terrible things. I guess I was. . . afraid to feel so much. No matter what I did, you were still there. And now that I've found you, I can't imagine being without you. I've done so many unthinkable things that I regret. . ." His voice broke at this point. "But you make me feel like it's all okay. That it doesn't matter. That I can get past it."

She was fading. . . and he could feel it. "Please. . ." she whispered weakly, "Don't stop. . ."

He drew in a shuddering breath. "I can't think about tomorrow without thinking of you. When I look into your eyes, I see my life. I see my future. My atrocious deeds are washed away. Where I come from, I'm a prince."

"You're *my* prince," she whispered even more quietly.

He raised one of his hands and wiped away his tears. "I have wealth and power. I could have anything I want there. . . but you're *here*. . . and you are *all* I'll ever want."

Gwyn didn't reply.

He held her tightly to him unable to control his sobs. He didn't want to die. He wanted to be with her. His family didn't acknowledge God, but Kael was praying to Him now. . . praying that he would die quickly. . . praying that they could be together in death.

His mind was calm as his arms loosened around Gwyn. His eyelids grew heavy and his breaths were few and far between. Finally, with some sense of peace, he drew his last breath.

It was all so quiet. Everyone was dead. The only sound was the wind demanding to know why so much blood had been spilt on the earth. Liza demanded the answer to that herself. She had always seen violence as entirely unnecessary. Clearly, her parents thought differently.

She wandered through the quiet field having to step and trip over the dead bodies. Her shoes were resistant to the blood. She was glad for that because she wouldn't be able to stand the feeling.

She walked until she found the cabin in the woods knowing that she would find Kael there. She stepped inside to see that the fire they had built had already burned out. There was the faint smell of smoke and ash and the strong smell of the crimson liquid that was drying on the bodies.

They were still holding each other. She wasn't sure that she had ever seen anything so sad and so beautiful. She would always be proud of Kael for his humanity. He showed her that it was alright to feel. It was alright to be selfless. It was alright to have compassion for humans. He had accomplished so much considering what her parents made turn him into.

Her tears stung her dry eyes. She knew what needed to be done. She didn't care what happened to her afterwards. She was given one of the most unique gifts known throughout her race. . . it was time to use it for something that was purely good.

Liza closed her eyes as her body was consumed by light. It extracted from her and set a glow around her figure. The field began to glow as she did. The area was surrounded by a white light. This light hovered over the bodies for a moment then slowly sank into them.

One by one, the people stirred. Their wounds had healed. They were breathing again. When she was sure that they were all alive, she used her other not-so-unique abilities to place all the humans safely in their homes, dressed in pajamas, and feeling ready to wake up and start the day.

The aliens got to their feet. They knew what had happened. Though they were annoyed that the humans had also been given life, they were relieved that *they* were alive. They returned to their ship and Liza was able to finish the job. She erased what had happened on the field.

Allison sat up on the cold floor of the basement blinking in amazement. Johnny sat up next to her tilting his head in confusion.

"Did we fall asleep?" he asked her.

She knew that it had happened differently, but she nodded. "Yes. . . I think we did."

Johnny stretched out his arms and yawned tiredly, his eyes still wanting to rest. "What should we do now?"

"Well. . ." She was trying to figure out why they were alive. She didn't know how and she didn't know why. . . not that it mattered. They were *alive*. By some miracle, they were breathing again. Their wounds were healed and the blood had disappeared from their clothes. "I guess we'll wait here for Gwyn."

"Kael too?"

Oh. . . she hadn't thought about that. Surely if *they* had been brought back, then Kael and Gwyn would be alright. "Yes. Kael too."

Gwyn's eyes opened. She thought she was dead for a moment. Then she saw that Kael was still there, so it must have meant. . . that. . . what? Were they still breathing? No, she was sure that she had died. Did that mean that Kael was dead? Then she heard his heart beating. He was alive — and so was she.

They both got to their feet unsure of their surroundings. They shouldn't have been getting up at all. Gwyn looked down at her stomach searching for her fatal wound. But it wasn't there. Neither was the blood. She looked at Kael to see that he was as good as new too.

"What did you do?" Kael asked in a quiet voice.

Liza smiled at them. "Everyone who died has been revived. Gwyn, your kind doesn't remember what happened. *Our* kind does. The only humans who know are you and Allison."

Gwyn's heart skipped a beat. She had almost forgotten about her cousin. "Then Allison and Johnny. . . they're okay?"

Liza nodded. "They are now."

Kael couldn't express how grateful he was to his sister, but it showed in his eyes. Liza had always understood him. "Thank you." He wrapped his arms around her and kissed her cheek.

"You're welcome," she grinned with tears still in her eyes, "Now go. . . carpe diem."

He let out a slow breath. He had taken breathing for granted before; it was cleansing to do it now.

Kael took Gwyn's hand and walked with her outside. They went back through the trees and returned to the field watching the sun shine brightly in the sky.

He looked over at Gwyn who had the most beautiful smile on her face. It was something he had missed and something that he knew he would never miss again. She looked back at him and gave his hand a tight squeeze. A new day had begun with a miracle.

***

Gwyn didn't know how to tell the president that the battle had already happened, but she would have to sooner or later. Her parents already knew. She had told Allison everything. Though they told Johnny about the battle, they agreed that Johnny didn't need to know that he and Allison had died. Perhaps they would tell him when he was older.

Liza decided to live on earth. She felt that she could do good there. Their parents were furious and blamed Kael. They would never understand and she didn't particularly care. Earth was the place to be. It wasn't perfect, but it felt like home.

Gwyn blinked awake; the sun was shining through the curtains. She would have been very annoyed with the sun, but she was still in the wonderment of being alive. "Are you awake?"

Kael kissed her shoulder before sitting up. "I am now."

"What time is it?" She sat up next to him, scratching her head as she looked for the time on her clock. "Oh. . . it's after noon."

"I guess they let us sleep in."

They dragged themselves out of bed and got ready for the day with smiles on their faces. Their stomachs were growling, but they were ignored. They wanted to get outside and see everyone.

Allison, Johnny, and Liza were in the pool. They had gotten one in the backyard as soon as they could. It didn't make sense to go to Allison's house just to use the pool.

"Hey, sleepy-heads!" Johnny grinned at them. "Are you coming in?"

"Not yet," Gwyn answered. "We need to wake up first."

Johnny shrugged and went back to bouncing a beach ball off of Liza's head.

Kael kissed the top of Gwyn's head. "I think the best part of all this was making up."

Gwyn giggled. "I agree." As she fiddled with the engagement ring on her finger and contemplated changing into her bikini, she heard footsteps behind them.

Katherine hugged Gwyn and smiled approvingly at Kael, then she headed into the pool. They had spoken several times since she'd informed them of what really happened. They seemed to be happy – which was nice – though Joseph hadn't said much since.

He stood by the pool for a moment before he turned to Kael and held out his hand. "I want to apologize. . . for my behavior throughout this whole ordeal. I can't stay that I'll be able to forget what happened to my children. . . but I can accept that you are going to be my daughter's husband. It's clear to me that you're not the same person that you were. . . you're a good man."

Kael smiled. Joseph had called him a *man*. He couldn't have said anything better. "Apology accepted." He shook Joseph's hand with pride.

Joseph went into the pool and stood beside his wife giving her the most loving kiss that Gwyn had ever seen him give her. It made her heart flutter.

Everyone was swimming except them. They were just looking at their family. They were all happy – and they were all together.

"It's nice to see them at peace," Kael said as he put his arm around her shoulder.

"Well, there's going to be one more person that we'll have to keep happy," Gwyn smiled.

He looked down at her knowing what she meant but wanting her to tell him. She took his other hand and placed it on her stomach. Kael grinned happily and her smile widened. It could not have happened at a better time.